Matt paused in front of her

"Are we going to talk about it? Or are you going to pretend it doesn't exist?"

"Talk about what?" She tilted her head to make eye contact.

"This." He leaned in and brushed his lips across hers, then pulled away—too soon.

Her heart stumbled, then regained its balance as she quickly scanned the area, fearing one of the locals had witnessed the kiss. Thank goodness they were alone in the parking lot.

"We're attracted to each other," he said.

She shook her head.

"Deny it all you want, Amy. But it's there in your eyes."

Lord help her, she was in deep.

Dear Reader,

This year Harlequin Books celebrates its 60th anniversary—congratulations Harlequin!

I came across my first Harlequin book while waiting in a dentist office over twenty years ago. I've been hooked ever since. What I love most about Harlequin romances is the guaranteed "Feel-Good Sigh" at the end of every book. I'm especially fond of the Harlequin American Romance line, where everyday people from all walks of life, small towns or big cities, find their very own Happy-Ever-Afters. The characters in these stories often experience the same day-to-day struggles many readers deal with—working, raising children and juggling finances. A Harlequin American Romance book reminds us of what's really important in the grand scheme of life—family, friends and love. I consider it a privilege to write for Harlequin and hope *A Cowboy's Promise* leaves you with a "Feel-Good Sigh."

For more information on my books please visit www.marinthomas.com, or contact me at marin@marinthomas.com. For the most current news on Harlequin American Romance releases and their authors visit www.harauthors.blogspot.com.

Happy reading!

Marin Thomas

A Cowboy's Promise

Marin Thomas

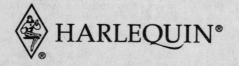

HARLEQUIN®

TORONTO • NEW YORK • LONDON
AMSTERDAM • PARIS • SYDNEY • HAMBURG
STOCKHOLM • ATHENS • TOKYO • MILAN • MADRID
PRAGUE • WARSAW • BUDAPEST • AUCKLAND

Recycling programs
for this product may
not exist in your area.

ISBN-13: 978-0-373-75257-7
ISBN-10:   0-373-75257-1

A COWBOY'S PROMISE

Copyright © 2009 by Brenda Smith-Beagley.

www.eHarlequin.com

Printed in U.S.A.

ABOUT THE AUTHOR

Typical of small-town kids, all Marin Thomas, born in Janesville, Wisconsin, could think about was how to leave after she graduated from high school.

Her six-foot-one-inch height was her ticket out. She accepted a basketball scholarship at the University of Missouri in Columbia, where she studied journalism. After two years she transferred to University of Arizona at Tucson, where she played center for the Lady Wildcats. While at Arizona, she developed an interest in fiction writing and obtained a B.A. in radio-television. Marin was inducted in May 2005 into the Janesville Sports Hall of Fame for her basketball accomplishments.

Her husband's career in public relations has taken them to Arizona, California, New Jersey, Colorado, Texas and Illinois, where she currently calls Chicago her home. Marin can now boast that she's seen what's "out there." Amazingly enough, she's a living testament to the old adage "You can take the girl out of the small town, but you can't take the small town out of the girl." Her heart still lies in small-town life, which she loves to write about in her books.

Books by Marin Thomas

HARLEQUIN AMERICAN ROMANCE
1024—THE COWBOY AND THE BRIDE
1050—DADDY BY CHOICE
1079—HOMEWARD BOUND
1124—AARON UNDER CONSTRUCTION*
1148—NELSON IN COMMAND*
1165—SUMMER LOVIN'
        "The Preacher's Daughter"
1175—RYAN'S RENOVATION *
1184—FOR THE CHILDREN **
1200—IN A SOLDIER'S ARMS**
1224—A COAL MINER'S WIFE**
1236—THE COWBOY AND THE ANGEL

  *The McKade Brothers
**Hearts of Appalachia

Each year since 2005 the U.S. Senate has passed a resolution designating the fourth Saturday of July **National Day of the American Cowboy.**

"Pioneering men and women, recognized as cowboys, helped establish the American West...that cowboy spirit continues to infuse the nation with its solid character, sound family values and good common sense; the cowboy embodies honesty, integrity, courage, compassion, respect, a strong work ethic and patriotism."

Whether he wears a military or blue-collar uniform or suit and tie to work, if you look closely there's a little bit o' cowboy in every American man.

Long Live the Cowboy!

Chapter One

"He's still out there, Mama," Amy Olson's seven-year-old daughter, Rose, announced from her perch on the chair in front of the kitchen window.

Ten minutes earlier, a shiny black 4x4 extended-cab pickup towing a luxury horse trailer large enough to comfortably transport six animals pulled up the gravel drive. Amy hadn't caught the license plate, but she doubted the driver was from Pebble Creek—no one in this area made enough money raising horses to purchase such a spiffy vehicle. But unlike her neighbors in the small eastern Idaho Valley, Amy was barely hanging on to her land much less making ends meet.

Positive she was viewing a mirage Amy tugged her blouse loose from the waistband of her jeans and rubbed the hem of the cotton material against the windowpane in front of her daughter's nose. The shirt came away smudged with dust. When was the last time she'd cleaned, let alone washed windows? She glanced at the wall calendar and sighed. She'd tidied the house right before Christmas—five months ago.

The lone cowboy sat inside his truck, yakking on a

cell phone. He looked toward the house once or twice, but mostly he stared out the windshield, grinning and gesturing with his arms. Then his head fell back and his shoulders shook. Whoever was on the other end of the call sure tickled his funny bone. Go figure. Amy didn't find the cowboy or his fancy rig amusing.

As a matter of fact she'd lost her sense of humor—what there had been of it anyway—when the owner of her last boarded horse removed the animal from her farm a week earlier, drying up her sole source of income.

Who is he and what business does he have with the Broken Wheel?

"Is he lost, Mama?"

Lord, I hope so. She wasn't in the mood for a visit from one of her husband's creditors.

Since when do collection agencies send their henchmen out in diesel pickups towing horse trailers?

The truck door opened and Amy held her breath. A Stetson emerged. Then a pair of broad shoulders. She estimated his height to be around one or two inches over six feet. He moved around the hood and her first head-to-toe glance triggered a mini-heart attack.

Amy had a weakness for cowboys.

He paused midstride and her ticker resumed beating. His head turned toward the barn, revealing a strong jaw and a wide mouth, which wasn't smiling now. After a moment, he swaggered—that's how most cowboys, who believed they were God's gift to women, walked— over to the house. He took the porch steps two at a time and instead of ringing the bell he pounded.

"Go upstairs and check on Lily," she ordered her

daughter. "But don't wake her if she's napping. And stay in your room until I call for you."

Rose obeyed, grabbing the box of Cheerios off the kitchen table—her sister's favorite food—before leaving the kitchen. Amy unconsciously brushed at her bangs. When she caught her reflection in the window, she grimaced. *Do you really care what the man thinks of you?*

No, she did not. She'd transferred handsome cowboys to her been-there-done-that list several years ago.

When she opened the door, cool blue eyes pinned her. Mesmerized, she gaped, uncaring if the man considered her behavior rude. A split-second fantasy flashed through her mind—she and the cowboy lying in a field of clover beneath a cornflower-colored sky— which slowed her thundering pulse to a sluggish *thump thumpity thump.*

"Ma'am."

The deep voice abruptly ended the dream. "May I help you?" she squeaked.

He removed his hat.

She wished he hadn't.

Strands of dark hair, the color of the dirt after a hard rain, lay every which way across his brow and over the tips of his ears, lending him a shaggy beach-bum appeal. She easily pictured the cowboy in Hawaiian-flowered swim trunks surfing an ocean wave. Then he smiled.

Good Lord. He was a heartbreaker.

Soul-stopper.

Woman-dropper.

His gaze swept her from head to toe, its indifference

almost insulting. Amy wasn't a looker—at least for the past several months she hadn't been one. Each morning the bathroom mirror reminded her that she had an inch of dark roots showing. But money was tight and she didn't dare waste a penny on a cut and color. Besides, a trip to the hair salon wouldn't erase the worry lines that had taken up residence across her forehead the past few months.

"Matt Cartwright." He offered his hand.

His fingers were marked by thick calluses and a scar bisected his palm—a bad rope burn, she suspected. He shifted, the movement sending shards of afternoon sunlight ricocheting off the silver belt buckle at his waist. According to the inscription—Dodge National Circuit Finals Rodeo—the man was an authentic rodeo cowboy. *Figures.* Rodeo cowboys were useless. She ought to know—she'd married one.

Steeling herself, she clasped his hand, ignoring the jolt of awareness that spread through her. Holy smokes, her breasts were tingling. When was the last time *that* had happened?

"I've got business with Ben Olson."

He hadn't heard? Amy's attention shifted to the horse trailer. "Ben's not here."

"Any idea when he'll be back?"

"Not soon." *That was for sure.*

Mr. Cartwright rubbed his chin, dragging his fingers across the emerging five o'clock shadow, the scratchy noise too intimate a sound between them for having just met. "I dialed his cell phone numerous times, but he never answered. Then a few weeks ago the number was no longer in use."

That's because Amy hadn't been able to pay the wireless phone bill and the company had cancelled her service. "Maybe I can help," she said.

Brow furrowed, he shifted his weight from one boot to the other. "I'm sorry, who are you?"

"Amy Olson. Ben's wife." His eyes rounded—evidently he hadn't been aware that Ben had been married. "Would you like to leave a message for my husband?" she asked, hoping to buy a few weeks before he figured out the truth.

"Actually, I'd like to leave three of my mares with him."

"Excuse me?"

Dark eyebrows curved inward over his nose—a nose that had been broken at least once according to the bump along its bridge. "Did your husband happen to mention a business agreement he made with me?"

Damn her pie-in-the-sky, dreaming, scheming husband. She pushed the words past her lips. "He did not."

The cowboy rocked on his boot heels, clearly agitated by the lack of progress in their conversation. "Ben and I met in Pocatello this past December."

Not surprising. Her husband had chased the rodeo dream since before they'd married. If Ben wasn't competing, he was in the stands cheering. But he'd never been good enough to win a buckle like this cowboy. A sliver of dread crawled up Amy's spine. She hoped to heaven that the deal her husband had struck with this man had nothing to do with the beast in the barn. "I'm listening."

"On the eve of the National Finals Rodeo a group of cowboys organized a poker game and—"

"The short version. I have chores to do." Not true. Few tasks remained on the farm since her horse-boarding business had gone belly-up. Regardless, she wanted this cowboy gone—yesterday.

"The short version, Mrs. Olson, is that your husband lost to me at poker and I'm here to collect on his debt."

Blast it, Ben. Her husband had no business playing cards. He couldn't keep a straight face if his life depended on it. As a matter of fact he couldn't walk straight, sleep straight, sit straight or talk straight. He'd been the most wishy-washy man she'd ever met. "How much does Ben owe you?"

"Thirty-thousand."

A high-pitched buzz whistled between her ears. She opened her mouth but only air rushed out.

"Since your husband wasn't able to procure the funds we struck a bargain."

"Bargain?" she wheezed.

"Free stud service in lieu of the money he owes me."

That surely wasn't going to happen. Besides… "Most serious horse breeders prefer artificial insemination."

His devilishly wicked grin revealed a perfect set of pearly whites. "Call me old-fashioned, but I believe a lady who's been properly courted behaves better in the bedroom, er…stall, I mean."

If she squeezed the doorknob any tighter, she'd bust the hardware. "I'm sorry about the gambling debt, but you can't leave your horses here." She attempted to slam the door in his face, but a size-thirteen Roper blocked the way. He held out a piece of paper.

No mistaking Ben's handwriting. She scanned the

contents. The message said exactly what Mr. Cartwright claimed—free stud service for three mares valued at thirty thousand dollars—except her husband was to have delivered Son of Sunshine over a month ago to the Lazy River Ranch outside Tulsa, Oklahoma. "Like I said…can't help you." When he made no move to take the note, she stuffed it into his shirt pocket, ignoring the hard wall of flesh that her knuckles nudged.

"Mrs. Olson, I'm not leaving until I speak with Ben."

The resentment and frustration that had been damned up all these months burst free, sending a flood of anger rushing through her. "I'm afraid you'll have yourself quite a long wait."

His eyes narrowed, leaving only a slice of blue visible. "And why's that?"

"Because Ben's dead."

The cowboy's mouth dropped. "Dead…dead?"

Was there any other kind? "Dead as in buried over yonder." She pointed to a grassy knoll a hundred yards beyond the barn—the family burial ground. Hard to miss her great-grandparents' headstone standing ten feet high. She motioned to the horse trailer. "I apologize for any inconvenience Ben may have caused you. Good day, Mr. Cartwright."

This time the door encountered no roadblock and closed with a bang!

Dead?

Ben Olson couldn't be dead. Matt had played cards with the bronc rider this past December at the Holt Arena on the campus of Idaho State University. Although they'd run into each other at rodeos through the years, Matt hadn't known the man well, save for the fact that he had a reputation for gambling—and losing. The way Olson flirted with the rodeo groupies, Matt would never have believed the man had been married. And speaking of wives...

The widow sure hadn't acted torn up over the loss of her husband. Unless...had he been duped by the couple?

He smashed his Stetson on his head and headed up the hill to the graveyard encased behind a three-foot wrought-iron fence, its rusted finials pointing heavenward. With long strides he covered the ground, spewing cuss words in sync with the gravel bits flying out from beneath his boot heels. He refused to entertain the possibility that his plan to retire from rodeo had encountered a roadblock he was unable to swerve around. He stopped outside the gate and scanned the handful of granite markers. Ben...Ben...Ben...

Oh, hell.

Benjamin Olson

Loving Husband and Father

Matt shifted his attention from the grave marker to the rolling green hills that butted up to the jagged peaks of the southern end of the Teton Mountain Range. His first thought—nice place to be buried. Second thought—*now what?* It had been evident by the daze on Amy Olson's face that her husband had failed to mention he'd lost thirty thousand dollars in a poker game.

When Matt had discovered that Olson had recently purchased the famous American quarter horse Son of Sunshine, Matt had been consumed with the idea of breeding his mares with the stallion. At eight years of age the stud was regarded as one of the top-ten cutting horses in the country.

Blame it on karma, kismet or providence, but Matt believed running into Olson at the National Finals Rodeo had been a signal that the time was right for the career change Matt had contemplated for months—raising cutting horses. To begin his new venture with offspring sired by Son of Sunshine was an opportunity Matt hadn't been able to pass up.

The cutting-horse operation was to be a turning point in Matt's life, allowing him to retire from rodeo. He remained a contender—one of the top tie-down cowboys on the Prairie Circuit. But at the age of thirty-four he was tired of life on the road, sleeping in dingy motels and eating fast food day in and day out.

In truth, he'd been ready to walk away from the sport when he'd turned thirty. But back then he hadn't known what he'd wanted to do with the rest of his life—except that he didn't relish working for his father in the oil business. Matt preferred the smell of a rank barn to thick black crude.

His agreement with Olson had stated that the man was to deliver the stud to his father's ranch in Oklahoma by the end of April. April had faded into May and no sign of the stud and no contact with Olson.

The clock had been ticking. The mares' natural breeding season was May through September. When the first week of May had passed and Olson remained a no-show, Matt had taken matters into his own hands and hauled his horses to Idaho.

From his vantage point on the hill the old homestead left a lot to be desired. The shabby two-story white clapboard—most of the paint had peeled off over the years—listed to the left as if the steady Idaho winds were trying to shove it off its foundation. The shutters had faded from glossy black to dull charcoal, and one shutter was missing from a second-story window. Olson hadn't put any money into upkeep. Not unusual. Most ranchers and horse breeders sunk their profits into their operations.

Next Matt eyed the horse barn—in slightly better condition than the house—and the empty paddocks. Dread settled like a hot road apple in the pit of his stomach. Had the widow sold off the prized stallion?

Guess he'd better find out. Matt returned to the house and stomped up the porch steps. The door opened unexpectedly and he had to yank his arm back to prevent his knuckles from rapping the widow's forehead.

"Need more proof Ben's dead, Mr. Cartwright?" Her nose wrinkled as if she'd caught a whiff of a foul odor—*him*.

Was her testy demeanor the result of her husband's death or just her normal pleasing personality? First things first. He removed his hat. "My condolences on the loss of your husband."

His apology sucked the hissy-fit out of her. Her brown eyes softened to the color of well-oiled saddle leather as she murmured, "Thank you."

When they'd spoken earlier, he hadn't paid attention to her face. She seemed too damned young to be a widow—clear skin, nondescriptive features and a cap of blondish bouncy curls that bobbed in every direction when she moved her head. She was average height—somewhere between five-five and five-six with curvy hips and plenty of eye-catching bosom. Not that he had any interest in her figure.

He shored up his defenses. He'd learned the hard way that the opposite sex usually possessed an agenda. He'd been burned once by a needy female and refused to walk that road again. And Amy Olson, her brown eyes brimming with bleakness, was the epitome of a woman in need.

"I'm hoping we can reach an agreement regarding your husband's debt."

"You must be joking."

Molars clamped together he pulled in a deep breath through his nose. The oxygen shot straight to his brain, clearing his head. "The way I see it, you have two choices, ma'am." He doubted she'd accept either one, but what the hell. "You pay me thirty thousand dollars or I leave my mares here and retrieve them at the end of the summer. Take your pick."

Eyelashes fluttering like hummingbird wings, she protested. "I don't have the means to care for your horses."

"Fine. I'll take a check."

She swept her arm across her body. "Does it look like I have thirty grand lying around, Mr. Cartwright?"

Score one for the widow.

"Might I suggest you sell off a few assets to free up the money?"

Her fingers latched on to her throat and he wasn't sure if she'd intended to halt the gasp that escaped her mouth or to choke herself to death. "I've got nothing left save the house and the land and that's not for sale."

Damn it all. Why didn't Amy Olson just brand the words *Help Me* across her forehead?

"Mama?"

Matt peeked around the door and spotted a dark-haired child holding a toddler with a mop of tangled blond curls. The curly-headed kid grinned around the thumb in her mouth, and a gush of drool spilled down her chin.

"Rose, honey, go upstairs."

The widow hadn't taken her eyes off him. He guessed her wariness indicated no other men occupied the premises. Right then the baby whimpered, and held chubby arms out to her mother. Tending to a grumpy kid trumped dealing with him.

"I'm going to unload my horses and leave them in the corral. We'll settle things in the morning." He'd made it as far as the bottom porch step when her words lassoed him.

"Nothing left to settle, Mr. Cartwright. Might as well be on your way."

"I'm not leaving the area until you pay off your husband's debt or grant me stud service." At her gasp, he clarified, "Stud service for my mares."

His ears winced when the door slammed shut.

"HE'S STILL OUT THERE, MAMA," Rose's same words echoed two hours later as the little girl stood sentry again at the kitchen window while Amy fixed supper. Following a snack of Cheerios, Lily had succumbed to another nap in the playpen, allowing Amy a rare moment of peace and quiet.

The baby had caught a cold, and the little princess

was fussier than usual. If Lily ended up with another ear infection, which she was prone to, Amy would have to take her daughter to the medical clinic in Rockton. She had no idea where she'd get the money to pay for the office visit. Ben's death had been a nasty monetary wake-up call.

The first few weeks she'd been numb. Then she'd gone into survival mode with one objective—keep the farm afloat. Now even that goal was slipping away. Reality had set in and Amy had to find a job to support her and the girls. Boarding horses was no longer an option—at least not until she decided what to do with that nasty stud in the barn.

"He sure does got pretty horses."

"Have, Rose. Not got," Amy corrected.

"Butch says *got* all the time and his mama don't, I mean, doesn't yell at him."

"I'm not yelling." Amy rolled her eyes. "And Butch knows better." The boy was their nearest neighbor's son. He and Rose shared the same first-grade teacher.

Rose puffed against the pane until it fogged over, then drew *B+R* with a heart around the letters. Her daughter was in the throes of her first crush.

"Quit messing up the window and set the table, please." Amy slathered butter on stale bread slices, then glanced over her shoulder and noticed too many dishes on the table. "Only three plates, Rose."

Ben's hazel eyes gazed at Amy from her daughter's face. "What about Daddy's friend?"

Daddy's friend had been how she'd explained Matt Cartwright's unexpected visit. "As soon as his horses rest up, he'll leave." She slapped cheese slices on the bread, set the sandwiches in the hot skillet, then wandered over to the window.

Her daughter was right. The mares were beautiful—American quarter horses. Two were buckskins, their yellowish-gold coats popping against glossy black manes, tails and lower legs. The other mare was chestnut with a burnished hide and a brownish-red mane and tail. Forcing her eyes away from the animals she studied the cowboy.

Matt.

Ben.

What was it about men with one-syllable names? Matt was easy on the eyes like Ben had been. And where had lusting after Ben gotten her? Screwed—literally. She'd best keep her eyeballs in her head and figure out a way to run Matt Cartwright off.

Damn you, Ben. Thirty thousand dollars? Her husband had insisted he'd gotten a handle on his gambling addiction. Or maybe she'd just yearned to believe him. Stupid. Stupid. Stupid.

While she flipped the sandwiches, she mentally calculated the bills piling up. Her May mortgage payment was overdue, which ignited her fanny on fire. The land had belonged to her mother's side of the family for four generations. Her parents had managed to pay off the farm before they'd drowned in a boating accident a few years ago. Because Ben had accumulated a substantial amount of gambling debt, she'd consented to taking out a second mortgage on the property to pay off his losses—under the condition he attend Gamblers Anonymous. He'd agreed.

Instead of repaying off the huge cash advances he'd

taken out against several credit cards, her husband had purchased Son of Sunshine and had gambled away the rest. When he'd shown up at the farm with the stallion he'd lied and claimed he'd fallen off the wagon and had used his poker winnings to buy the stud.

If that wasn't insult enough, Ben had had the nerve to up and die, leaving her with credit card debts, a sixteen-hundred-dollar-a-month mortgage and a stud whose unpredictable behavior had caused her horse-boarding clients to flee, leaving her with no source of income.

She'd sold off her great-great-grandmother's rare 1860's Patent Williams & Orvis Treadle Sewing Machine for $2,495.00 to clear one of the credit cards, but that hadn't made a dent in the thousands of dollars of debt remaining. If she had the opportunity to sell the stud she would. But who in their right mind would shell out big bucks for a dangerous horse?

"He's hungry," Rose said.

Amy lowered the flame under the burner, then peeked over her daughter's shoulder. The cowboy unloaded a hay bale from the pickup bed and spread it around the corral. Then he wandered over to the stock tank, peered inside and shook his head. No sense keeping fresh water in the reservoir after her boarding business had dried up. He turned on the spigot and filled the trough. "How can you tell he's hungry?" Amy asked.

"'Cause he's a good worker."

Wouldn't it be nice if all life's questions came with such simple answers? Sandwiches done, she sliced an apple, delivered the meal to the table and poured Rose a glass of milk. "Wash your hands. I'll be right back."

Amy left the house and crossed the drive to where the cowboy stood with one boot propped on the lower rung of the corral, arms folded across the top, watching the mares race about, kicking up dust. "Your horses are spectacular."

He turned his head and his eyes sucked her into a vortex of swirling blue. How easy it would be to fall under this man's spell. "I'm truly sorry about your husband's death," he said.

Even though the words were sincere, she'd had enough of pitying looks and mumbled sympathies. It wasn't easy being reminded how gullible she'd been. Besides, *I'm sorry* wouldn't pay the mortgage or breathe life into her dead husband. "We're having grilled cheese sandwiches for supper. You're welcome to join us."

His lips curled at the corners. "Thanks all the same, but I'll grab a bite to eat in town."

Rude man. She hugged herself, because the wind had picked up, not because the cowboy had declined her meal invitation. "You're not going to make this easy on me and disappear, are you?"

"No, ma'am, I'm not."

"If you don't mind me saying—" she gestured to his horse trailer "—you appear to have the financial means to absorb a thirty-thousand-dollar loss."

"That's beside the point. A deal is a deal. I intend to breed my mares to Son of Sunshine."

Enough said. There would be no changing the wrangler's mind—not today. She spun, but he stopped her with a hand on her shoulder. "How did Ben die?"

She supposed he had a right to know. "He was attacked by a horse."

The wind died suddenly, as if heaven held its breath. "What horse?" he asked.

"Son of Sunshine."

If she hadn't been watching his mouth she would never have heard his faintly uttered cuss word.

Shit.

Chapter Two

A smart man would understand when to stop pursuing a lost cause.

A smart man would know when to pull up stakes and hit the road.

At the moment Matt Cartwright didn't give a crap about how smart he was or wasn't.

As he drove away from the Broken Wheel late Saturday afternoon, he glanced in the rearview mirror. After issuing a supper invitation both Amy Olson and Matt knew he'd refuse, the widow stood in the gravel drive, shielding her eyes against the sun's glare, watching the truck's taillights fade into the distance.

When he reached the county road he pulled onto the shoulder and cut the engine. The anger he'd experienced at having his plans to breed his mares suspended was nothing compared to the shame consuming him.

It might not make sense, but Matt wasn't able to shake the feeling that one stupid poker game—instigated by him—had set in motion a series of events that had culminated with Ben's death. What if the card game had never taken place—would the future have played out differently? Would Ben be alive today?

Matt wanted to believe that if he'd been aware Olson had had a wife he'd never have suckered the compulsive gambler into playing poker.

Don't kid yourself. You would have done anything to gain access to Son of Sunshine.

He tilted the rearview mirror and stared himself in the eye. Had Kayla's betrayal left him with more than a broken heart and his pride in shreds? Had he channeled his hurt into a ruthless determination that ignored everyone and anything, including his own moral code?

Leave it alone, man. What's done is done. Matt would have to deal with the wreckage left behind from his own selfish interests—a widow, two fatherless girls and a prizewinning stud whose behavior had become unpredictable and erratic.

What the hell was he going to do now? His father disapproved of Matt's plans to enter into the horse-breeding business, and Matt didn't relish the idea of returning to Oklahoma with his tail tucked between his legs.

You're an ass—wallowing in self-pity while Amy Olson struggles to pick up the pieces after her husband's death.

What was it about the young widow that got to Matt—not her looks, that's for sure. Amy Olson didn't come close to the sexy groupies that pestered him on the road. She was a living, breathing, walking advertisement for home and hearth—kids included. A world of hurt and stubborn pride shone in her brown eyes, yet she carried herself—shoulders stiff, chin high—as if ready to face her next test, which happened to be him.

Fingers drumming the steering wheel, he considered his options. His stomach gurgled with hunger, so he started the truck and merged onto the highway, heading north into town. Five minutes later he slowed to a stop at the sole intersection in Pebble Creek.

The quaint map dot consisted of one city block of 1920's brick-front businesses. Fake, old-fashioned hitching posts lined the sidewalk. A livestock tank overflowing with red and purple flowers sat by the door of a beauty shop called Snappy Scissors Hair Salon. Mendel's Drug emporium offered a park bench for customers outside its store. Smith Tax Consultants was sandwiched between the beauty shop and drugstore. Farther down Wineball Realty had been painted in white lettering across a black awning. And at the end of the block sat United Savings and Loan.

Situated across the street was a turn-of-the-century Victorian home that had been converted into a tavern. *Joe's* was scrawled in red paint across the front window and a Michelob sign hung from the flagpole bracket mounted on the overhang of the porch. A pot of faded plastic daisies decorated the bottom porch step and two battered aluminum chairs graced either side of the front door. An orange tabby rested in a windowsill on the second floor.

Roxie's Rustic Treasures occupied the abandoned gas station on the corner. The treasures: iron headboards, broken furniture and an assortment of tools and dishes were scattered about the parking lot. Next to Roxie's, a life-size horse statue pawed the air in front of Pebble Creek Feed & Tack.

A sidewalk sign outside Pearl's advertised, Parking

in Rear, so Matt drove around the corner and swung into the lot behind the block of businesses. He left his hat on the front seat and entered through the back door of the diner, deciding he'd order a thick juicy burger.

"We're out of burger meat. Delivery truck jackknifed near Pocatello. Won't get here till morning," the waitress groused when she arrived to take his order at the lunch counter. The middle-aged woman with dyed blond hair scrutinized him through her mango-colored bifocals. "You're not from around these parts, are you?"

Matt read her name tag. "I'm from Oklahoma, Pearl."

"I met an Okie years ago. Didn't impress me none." She batted a set of false eyelashes.

"Maybe I'll change your mind." Matt's grin teased a twitch from the corner of the woman's mouth. "What do you recommend for a hungry cowboy?" He read the offerings scratched in white chalk on the blackboard mounted to the wall behind the counter.

"If you've a mind for home cooking try the meat loaf. Otherwise the Reuben ain't bad."

Pearl's World-Famous Meat Loaf... Matt shook his head. Every diner in America boasted a world-famous something. "Meat loaf it is and a cup of decaf."

"Sure thing."

After Pearl delivered his coffee, Matt forced his current dilemma to the far reaches of his mind and soaked up the atmosphere. Over the years he'd broken bread in plenty of small-town diners while traveling the circuit. After a while the mom-and-pop eateries blurred together. Pearl's business possessed candy-apple-red tabletops. Worn seats made from cheap leather that sported their share of cracks and splits, allowing the yellowed foam cushion inside to poke through.

Cigarette burns scarred the Formica lunch counter, which was the same red color as the booth tables. The wall facing the street displayed a collection of license plates from all corners of the United States—even Hawaii. Framed photographs hung near the door— famous people like the 1978 4-H Fair Queen and the 2007 school district spelling-bee champion. Instead of the custom jukebox in the corner wailing Gatlin Brothers' songs, the local farm bureau report droned from a radio at the end of the counter.

Snatches of conversation filtered into Matt's ear. A group of elderly women gossiped about the local pastor and traded apple pie recipes. A couple of hippies in their fifties, wearing tie-dyed T-shirts and torn jeans, shared an animated conversation—probably reminiscing over a recent biker rally. A middle-aged couple in a corner booth sat stone-faced over cups of coffee. And a trio of anglers nearby complained about the new state-wide limit on chinook salmon.

"Passin' through to the next go-round?" The question came from two stools away. Friendly gray eyes smiled out of a chiseled face covered in white whiskers. "Noticed the buckle." The geezer's arthritic pointer finger crooked at an odd angle.

"Here on business." Matt swiveled his stool and shook hands. "Matt Cartwright by way of Tulsa."

"Jake Taylor. Foreman out at the Gateway Ranch."

"Horses?" Matt guessed.

"Yes, sir. This here part of Idaho is horse country. What brings you to our neck of the woods?"

"I've got business with the Broken Wheel."

"How much you givin' Amy for the place?"

Hadn't Amy claimed her house and land weren't for sale? Matt didn't want to hear that Ben Olson's death was forcing his wife to sell out. "I'm not interested in her farm."

"Hope your business ain't with that stallion in the barn."

"It's true then? The horse attacked Olson?"

"Hard to say. Amy found Ben on the ground inside the stall with his chest caved in. Could be the stud went loco or could be it was a freak accident."

Matt winced as the scene played out in his mind. Most folks would refuse to take a chance on a stallion with volatile behavior, no matter how famous the stud. "I'm surprised she hasn't put the horse down."

"I reckon she's hopin' to sell the animal so she can hang on to the place." The old man slurped his coffee. "Amy ran a horse-boardin' business, but her customers up and left. Can't say I blame 'em. Wouldn't want my animal in the same barn as SOS—Ben's nickname for the stud."

"That's too bad." Matt had a weakness for underdogs, and the temptation to rescue the widow nagged him, but he doubted she'd appreciate his interference.

"She's a fighter, I'll give her that," Taylor continued. "But ain't no way she's gonna hang on to the farm without an income."

"Meat loaf should be up in a minute, cowboy," Pearl informed Matt as she topped off the men's mugs.

Jake nodded his thanks, then said, "A damned shame Payton Scott over at the bank's puttin' the squeeze on Amy."

Matt hated to hear that the local banker had ganged up on the widow. Whatever happened to small-town folk caring for their own?

"Heard tell," Pearl whispered, inviting herself into the conversation, "that Payton offered Amy a teller position, but she snubbed her nose at the position."

Why would the widow refuse the job? *Don't ask.* Matt remained silent, content to count the salt and pepper shakers lined up on the shelf behind the lunch counter.

"The farm's been in her mama's family for generations," Taylor grumbled.

After Pearl walked away, Matt felt compelled to keep the conversation going. "I met Ben in Pocatello at the NFR this past December."

"Ben had no business bustin' broncs. Amy swore he didn't stick to nothin', includin' a saddle. When he wasn't off chasin' rodeo dreams he mostly sat on his one-spot. Never did figure out why Amy's mama allowed her to hitch up with the lazy bum."

"Dig in." Pearl set the world-famous meat loaf in front of Matt, and a Rueben sandwich next to Taylor before heading to the cash register to ring up the hippies.

Matt studied the charred meat.

"Pearl's meat loaf tastes like rawhide." Taylor bit into the sandwich. "Try the Reuben next time."

Blah. Matt's displeasure must have shown on his face because the geezer chuckled and slid the ketchup bottle over.

For a few minutes the men gave talking a rest.

Matt's thoughts drifted to the argument he'd had with his father before he'd loaded up his mares and left Oklahoma. His sister, Sam, had accidentally blurted out Matt's plan to take a sabbatical from rodeoing at the supper table one evening and Matt had been forced to reveal his intent to breed his mares with SOS.

The old man had acted as if Matt had betrayed him and the discussion had escalated into a shouting match followed by his father's pledge to withhold Matt's trust fund until he joined Cartwright Oil and forgot his dream of raising cutting horses. Matt had thumbed his nose at his father's threat. After purchasing the three mares, he was slowly building his savings account up thanks to his winning streak on the rodeo circuit this past winter.

Damn it all to hell. He hated to return to Oklahoma and face an I-told-you-so from the old man. "Anybody ever get close to SOS after he attacked Ben?" Matt asked.

"Nope. Ain't nobody crazy enough to try."

Maybe he was nuts for believing he might be able to work with the stallion. There were a million and one reasons horses snapped. Had Ben mistreated Son of Sunshine? Matt didn't believe so. Ben had behaved with respect around rodeo stock the times Matt had observed him.

"Gotta run." Taylor retrieved his hat from the stool next to him and dropped it on his head. "Hope your business with the Broken Wheel gets resolved to your satisfaction." He shook hands with Matt, then left a dollar tip by his plate and shuffled out the door.

What to do now—load up his mares and head

home? Or convince the widow Olson to allow him to judge for himself if SOS was dangerous or not?

"Dessert, cowboy?" Pearl frowned at the half-eaten food on Matt's plate.

Afraid he'd offended the café owner, he assured, "It was great, Pearl. Guess I wasn't hungry." She rolled her eyes and slapped his meal ticket on the counter. "How's that Sleep-Ezee Motel out by the highway?" He added a five-dollar tip to his tab.

Pearl's mood brightened. "Arlene keeps the sheets clean."

"Any critters on the loose in the rooms?"

"Not that I ever heard of. Have a good one, cowboy," she said.

Now all Matt needed was a decent night's rest and a few more minutes with Amy to salvage this road trip and hopefully ease his conscience at the same time.

AMY STOOD ON THE PORCH Sunday morning watching the sunrise. Today she prayed the warm rays would lend her courage to face the handsome cowboy barreling up the drive.

She had to give him credit—unlike her husband Matt Cartwright was an early riser. Amy suspected beneath his cowboy-calendar good looks, the man was hardworking and determined. She both admired and resented those qualities.

Her single experience with rodeo cowboys had been her husband. Ben hadn't liked to toil too hard at anything. He preferred to spend his time searching for a pot of gold at the end of someone else's rainbow.

The rig stopped next to the horse trailer and the

cowboy marched her way. Today he wore work jeans—stonewashed and no discernable iron crease along the thigh like yesterday's pair. His western shirt was a tad faded and wrinkled. When he reached the porch steps, he paused. No smile, but he did tap his fingertips against the brim of his hat.

"Mornin'." The husky greeting poured over her like warm, sticky honey.

"Coffee?" Might as well be neighborly before she sent him and his mares packing.

"Appreciate that."

"Comin' right up." She set her mug on the rail and disappeared inside. No sense cozying up at the kitchen table. Matt Cartwright possessed the kind of presence that wouldn't fade after his body left the premises. The last thing she wanted in her home were reminders of the rodeo cowboy. She filled an extra-large mug with leaded brew and returned outside.

"Thanks." When he accepted the cup, his fingers nudged hers, setting off a series of explosive prickles along her nerve endings.

She collapsed on the top step—he remained at the bottom. Eye-to-eye. And boy, was he an eyeful of wrangler perfection.

Swaying sideways, he leaned against the handrail, then squinted into the steam rising from his mug. How often had she done that—stare into the brown liquid hoping the answers to life's questions would float to the top?

"I heard you board horses," he said.

"Not anymore. Thanks to that stud in the barn, folks are afraid to leave their animals on the property."

Matt focused on the mares in the corral and Amy took advantage of his preoccupation to study him. She began at his boots and worked her way north, making it as far as the faded-to-white patch of denim at his crotch when he asked, "Is it just you and the girls now that your husband's gone?"

She peeled her eyes from his jeans. This was her property—she had a right to peek at a man's you-know-what if she wanted. "My folks are gone now. Ben's mother lives in Kansas, but we never kept in touch with her." Amy had called Wynona to inform her of Ben's death, but all the old woman had to say was, "Don't surprise me none."

"It's not my place to pry—"

"Then don't."

He ignored her warning. "But it's apparent you've had a run of bad luck."

Seven years to be exact. Her bad luck had begun the day she'd married Ben. "My problems are none of your concern, Mr. Cartwright."

"Matt. Call me Matt, Amy."

The intimate sound of her name rolling off his tongue twisted her stomach into a knot.

"I'd like to strike a deal with you." He cleared his throat. "Give me one week to work with Son of Sunshine and if—"

"No." *Stupid man.* "I buried one cowboy because of that horse. Don't intend to bury another one."

Eyes flashing, he argued, "I've been around horses all my life—good ones and rotten-to-the-core ones. I'll know after a few days if SOS is loco or not."

"The proof's buried up the hill." She nodded toward the cemetery.

"Did anyone witness the horse attack your husband?"

Amy shook her head. She had no idea how long Ben had lain dying or dead. When he hadn't answered her calls for supper, she'd walked out to the barn and that's when she'd found him.

"There's a chance it might have been an accident."

"His chest was caved in, Mr. Cartwright. Whether it was an accident or not, the horse can't be trusted."

"My sister suffered a horse kick to the head when she was sixteen because the animal spooked while she was hosing it down. Something might have set SOS off and caught Ben unawares."

"Did your sister survive?"

"She did."

Matt didn't elaborate and Amy was afraid to ask if the woman suffered any lingering effects.

"One week," he pressed. "If the stud remains untouchable, I'll load up my mares and retreat to Oklahoma." He made it sound as if he was declaring war against the stallion.

She was tempted to give in because she hated the idea of euthanizing any animal unless it had been injured beyond help. But if anything happened to the cowboy, his death would be on her conscience. "No."

"SOS can save your farm."

The Pebble Creek gossipmongers were at it again. "Who says my farm needs saving?"

"Jake Taylor mentioned you were in danger of losing the place."

Jake Taylor meant well, but he talked too much.

"If I can prove that SOS didn't attack Ben, then you'd be able to sell the stud." He motioned to the house and the barn. "The money you'd make on the sale would go a long way in sprucing up the place."

He expected her to use the extra cash to beautify her home? Yeah, right. She'd pay off the rest of Ben's debts first and any money left over would be socked away for emergencies. "And if no one wants the horse after you've worked with him, what then?"

"Then I'll pay you what I can and take the stud off your hands."

Now she knew Matt Cartwright was crazy. His sober eyes studied her. Sweat tickled her scalp. And a red haze formed in her peripheral vision.

Pity. The damned cowboy felt sorry for her.

How dare he. How dare he act all chivalrous and cocky. She hadn't asked for his sympathy and darned if she'd allow him to play the white knight and rescue her.

But what if he can prove Ben's death was an accident? Dare she walk away from an opportunity to get out of debt sooner rather than ten years from now? "You're serious?"

"Dead serious." His mouth flattened and his eyes flicked toward the burial plot. "Sorry. I meant no disrespect."

"What happens if I waltz into the barn one morning and discover you've suffered the same fate as my husband?" The doctors had explained that the horse's kick had crushed Ben's ribcage and a splinter of rib bone had pierced his heart.

"Send my body back to Oklahoma and you can keep my mares, truck and rig for your trouble." He grinned.

Ha. Ha.

"I'm a tie-down roper. I've worked with horses all my life. I know the difference between an animal who's snapped and one who's been spooked or mishandled." When Amy remained silent, he added, "SOS is too valuable a horse not to be given a second chance before he's put down."

Oh, shoot. She'd believed all that compassion had been for show, but obviously the man intended to do the right thing for the stud. She wondered if he was also concerned with doing the right thing for her and the girls. "I can't afford feed and upkeep for the horses."

"I'll cover the costs for the animals and myself in exchange for hot showers and place to rest my head at night."

Was it her imagination or had his eyes strayed to her breasts when he'd mentioned resting his head somewhere? "I'm a woman alone with two children, Mr. Cartwright."

"I'll give you a list of references." He snapped his fingers. "As a matter of fact, call Jake Taylor over at the—"

"Gateway Ranch," she finished for him.

"Taylor and I ate supper at Pearl's last night."

Amy trusted the ranch foreman. Jake Taylor had been a close friend of her grandfather. If Jake had any doubts about Cartwright's character he'd tell her. "Excuse me a minute." She headed inside. A sheet of paper with Jake's cell number along with a dozen other neighbors' numbers was taped to the wall by the kitchen phone. Jake answered on the second ring.

"Hi, Jake, it's Amy."

"Hello, Amy. Everythin' okay out your way?"

"We're all fine. Listen, I'm calling about Matt Cart-wright."

"The rodeo cowboy?"

"Yes. He said you two met at Pearl's yesterday. He's asking for a chance to work with Son of Sun-shine." She left out the part about Matt wanting to stash his bedroll in her house. "Can I trust him?"

"I'd bet my best pair of ridin' gloves that he's a man of his word. Ain't nobody else willin' to get near that horse."

"I'm leaning toward giving him a shot," she admitted.

"Tell ya what, missy. I'll drop by soon and check on him."

Reassured, Amy said, "Thanks, Jake." After a brief goodbye she hung up.

An I-told-you-so grin greeted her when she stepped onto the porch. "Did I pass muster?"

"You passed." She bit the inside of her cheek to keep from smiling. She wished she possessed half the cow-boy's self-assuredness.

"Where should I stow my stuff?"

"The barn."

His face paled.

"You want to work with Son of Sunshine you might as well bunk with him, too." Amy swallowed a chuckle at his worried frown. "I'll loan you a pillow and a blanket for the cot in the tack room." She heard noises coming from the kitchen—the girls were up for the day. Halfway to the door, she stopped and issued a warning. "I wouldn't bother unpacking, Mr.—"

"Matt."

"I have a hunch you'll be calling it quits before day's end."

"We'll see about that, won't we? *Amy.*"

Chapter Three

Amy was upstairs digging through the linen closet while the girls played in their bedroom when the sound of crunching gravel filtered through the open window at the end of the hall. *He's back.* She cursed the ribbon of excitement that wound through her.

Earlier this morning after Matt had negotiated a week out of her, he'd fed and watered the horses, then had hopped into his truck and taken off. She shouldn't fret about where he went or what he did, but she caught herself watching the clock and counting the darned minutes until his return.

Arms loaded with sheets, blankets and a pillow, she closed the closet door with her boot heel. Right then the doorbell rang. She hurried to the stairs before she caught herself and stopped. What was she doing? Did she want Matt to believe she was so desperate for male attention that she'd come running each time he crooked a finger, rang a bell or called her name? Good grief, if she didn't watch herself around the cowboy she'd make a first-class fool out of herself a second time in her life.

Like her mother, Amy had fallen for a handsome face

merely to discover the man lacked substance. How many times over the years had she heard her mother grumble that Amy's father hadn't been good at anything save dreaming? Amy and her mother had worked their fingers to the bone caring for the boarded animals and tackling the chores around the farm while Amy's father piddled the days away writing down million-dollar ideas in a notebook that never left his side. Amy decided Matt could hold his horses—literally—and wait for her.

The doorbell rang again. "Mama," Rose poked her head into the hallway. "Want me to see who's here?"

"Thanks, honey. I'll get it." Amy took the stairs slowly—first one foot. Then the other. Next step. One foot, then the other. Next step. One foot, then the other…until she reached the landing. Deciding to set the sheets and blankets on the living-room couch she detoured through the dining room. By the time she'd refolded the linens, the cowboy had cooled his heels long enough.

Too long, evidently—Matt was nowhere in sight when she opened the door. Then she glanced down and gasped at the grocery bags arranged around the welcome mat. Lord, the man loved to eat. She wasn't sure she had room in the fridge for all the food. One by one she hauled the bags inside and dug through them. Silly Nilly fruit chews? Cap'n Crunch cereal? Macaroni and cheese? Powdered donuts? SpaghettiOs? This wasn't cowboy food. This was munchkin food.

The bags blurred before her eyes and a lump the size of a boulder formed in the middle of her throat. Matt had agreed to feed and water the horses and himself—not her and the girls, too. She swallowed hard, telling herself that his generosity had *ulterior motive* written all over it—he hoped to make it impossible for Amy to kick him off the place.

"Wow." Rose stood in the doorway, Lily at her side sucking her thumb.

"No thumb, Lily." Amy feared if her daughter didn't kick the nasty habit, she'd end up needing braces and there wouldn't be any money in the budget for orthodontic visits for years to come.

"Who got all this stuff?" Rose climbed onto a chair to watch the unpacking. Lily followed her sister's lead and claimed her own chair.

"Mr. Cartwright picked up a few things at the store for me." That wasn't a lie—not really. Besides, it wasn't either of her daughters' business who paid the grocery bill, which by the number of bags must have cost Matt a small fortune.

Lily spotted the bananas and clapped her hands. "Nanna! Me nanna!"

Amy washed a banana, peeled the fruit and handed it to Lily. "What would you like, Rose? Grapes?"

"Okay."

While the girls ate their snacks, she stowed the food. Good grief, Matt had purchased laundry detergent and a bottle of Mr. Bubble for bath time.

"Look, Lily!" Rose squealed, when she spotted the Silly Nilly box—fruit-chew snacks Amy had stopped buying when she'd tightened the budget.

"Lily, if you let Rose help you use the potty and wash your hands afterward, then you two can have a fruit chew and sit outside on the swing while I make supper."

"Okay." Lily stuffed the rest of the banana into her mouth, slid from the chair, then waddled off.

"She went, Mama," her eldest daughter announced five minutes later.

Amy crossed the room and straightened Lily's pants, then handed out the treats and warned, "Stay on the swing."

As soon as they stepped outside, Lily shouted, "Car!"

Not now. Payton Scott and his flashy red Mustang drove up the road. She followed the girls onto the porch and waited. The bank manager got out of his car and stood for a moment, staring at Matt's truck and horse trailer.

"What can I do for you, Payton?" Amy called.

A moment later he joined her on the porch. "Whose rig is that?"

She'd rather not discuss Matt in front of the girls. "C'mon in."

No sooner had the screen door closed than he demanded, "Whose horses are those?"

"They belong to Matt Cartwright. A friend of Ben's." Until she understood the reason for the visit, she refused to reveal any details of her and Matt's agreement. She motioned for her guest to sit. Payton chose to stand, one hand shoved deep into his trouser pocket. "What brings you by?" Amy asked.

"Bad news, I'm afraid."

"Oh?" She retrieved a cutting board and knife, then went to work chopping vegetables.

"I spoke with my father and he's decided against granting you a ninety-day reprieve on your mortgage payments."

"Why?" Amy had asked for the extension while she took a government-sponsored training class that began a week from tomorrow. The three-week data-entry program would hopefully lead to a job and a steady source of income until she figured out SOS's fate and resumed boarding horses. She'd hoped not to have to make a mortgage payment until September.

"You should have taken the job I offered you at the bank," Payton said, avoiding her question.

The job came with strings—strings that led right to Payton's bedroom. That's why she'd declined. Yes, she was desperate to keep her farm, but not desperate enough that she'd sleep with a potbellied pig. "I can't afford child care," she lied.

"I assumed you'd be stubborn, so the bank contacted Wineball Realty to begin the paperwork to put the property on the market."

Amy set the knife aside, lest she be tempted to use it on Payton rather than a tomato. "The farm isn't for sale."

He flashed a sinister smile. "It will be if you don't come up with the money for your May mortgage payment."

HIDDEN IN THE SHADOWS of the barn door, Matt had a clear view of Dapper Dan and his flashy sports car. Ignoring the girls, who'd been sitting on the porch swing, the visitor had followed Amy inside the house.

Matt had a hunch the man's visit wasn't a social call. *Don't get involved.* Shoot, Amy would tell him to butt out, too. He set the pitchfork aside and headed for the house, believing his curiosity about the visitor had to do with being neighborly and not territorial. He wouldn't intervene unless Amy wished him to, but at least she'd know he stood in her corner.

"Hello, ladies," Matt greeted the girls with a grin as he climbed the porch steps. The older child offered a solemn stare, but the toddler flashed a red-stained smile, then removed a half-chewed piece of food from her mouth and held it out. "Nilly."

They were eating the fruit snacks he'd purchased at the grocery store. "I don't believe we've officially met." He whipped off his hat and bowed. "Matt Cartwright. You can call me Mr. Matt." The older girl frowned. He wracked his brain, but her name slipped his memory. A flower. Yeah, that was it. Both girls were named after flowers. "So, Daisy—"

"Daisy's not my name."

He frowned. "Well, now, Daffodil, I—"

She giggled and shook her head. "Nope. I'm not Daffodil."

"Marigold?" he guessed.

"No, silly, I'm Rose."

"That's right—Rose." He snapped his fingers. "And your sister, Violet—"

More laughter, this time the toddler joined in and clapped her hands.

"I mean, Tulip."

"Her name's Lily."

Matt chuckled at their belly laughs. Drool dripped off the little one's chin and Rose's eyes twinkled. He was taken aback that a little kidding tickled the funny bones of a couple of pint-size cherubs. "I need to speak to your mother. You flower buds stay here."

He thought about knocking before entering the

house, then changed his mind when the visitor's raised voice carried through the screen door.

"You have no other option, Amy, but to sell."

"What's the reason your father won't allow me a grace period on my mortgage payment? The bank will hardly miss my sixteen hundred dollars each month."

"You're a bad risk."

"Ben was the bad risk. I'm not."

"You've got no income. No one's going to board horses here until you send that beast in the barn to the glue factory. Even that won't be enough. You've accumulated too much credit card debt."

"Ben's doing, not mine."

"Same difference."

Matt had heard enough. He entered the kitchen unannounced and crowded the banker's personal space. "Matt Cartwright." He held out his hand.

"Payton Scott."

Matt eyed Amy. She stood in front of the stove, her mouth stretched into a thin line. "It doesn't sound like Mrs. Olson is interested in selling at the moment."

Scott's brow furrowed. "Mrs. Olson is running out of options."

"The girls and I have nowhere to go, Payton. You can't kick me out of my own home."

Scott didn't bat an eyelash. The jerk had no qualms about putting a woman and her two daughters out on the street. "The farm is yours as long as you keep up with the payments."

"You didn't tell him?" Matt asked Amy, hoping she'd play along.

Scott's head bounced between Matt and Amy like a Ping-Pong ball. "Tell me what?"

"I'm paying Mrs. Olson a stud fee for Son of Sunshine." He rubbed his whiskered jaw. "What did we agree the fee would be again?"

The corner of her mouth twitched. "Sixteen hundred dollars."

"W-what?" Scott sputtered.

"You heard Mrs. Olson. Sixteen hundred dollars." He lowered his voice. "The exact amount of her mortgage."

Scott balled his hands into fists and straightened his shoulders until the buttons threatened to pop off his dress shirt. "You're wasting your money, mister. That horse is worthless." Scott stormed out. A minute later the Mustang motor revved and the banker sped off.

"Can we come in now?" Rose held Lily's hand on the other side of the screen door.

Matt pushed the door open and the girls went straight to Amy, wrapping their sticky hands around her legs. Had they sensed their mother's distress? Amy's mouth opened, then snapped shut. He came to her rescue. "What smells so good?"

"Fajitas. Supper will be ready in a few minutes. Bathroom's down the hall if you want to wash up."

He took one step, then stopped and considered his boots—boots that had been in a dirty barn all day. He returned outside and tugged off his Ropers, then padded through the narrow hallway.

The bathroom was the size of a closet—room for a sink and a toilet, nothing else. He squeezed in, shut the door and locked it, then sucked in a deep breath. He didn't condone men harassing women. Scott was nothing but a big bully.

After scrubbing his hands he bent over the sink and splashed water on his face. He hadn't signed on to be the widow's caretaker. All he wanted was to breed his mares with the stallion, then hit the road. So why did he have this annoying urge to protect the three females in the kitchen?

He'd rescued a needy female once before and that had blown up in his face. He was done with the white-knight routine. He'd make Amy's mortgage payment because it was the right thing to do and nothing more.

When he entered the kitchen, Rose was seated at the table—Lily in the high chair. "Where would you like me to sit?"

"Doesn't matter." Amy delivered a large bowl of stir-fried veggies and meat to the table.

Matt picked the chair between the two girls. Lily grinned. "Hi, you."

"Hi, you," he answered back.

Lily giggled.

"She always says that." Rose rolled her eyes.

Amy sat across from Matt. "Two-year-olds tend to repeat everything you say," she explained, then grabbed both her daughters' hands.

Head bowed, he waited. And waited. Then he cracked one eye. All three females stared at him. "What?"

"We're supposed to hold hands, Mr. Matt," Rose explained.

Feeling stupid, he gently grasped Rose's fingertips and darned if Lily didn't offer her chubby paw covered in baby spit.

"Lord, we ask that you bless this food and...bless Mr. Cartwright for providing us with groceries today. Amen."

He allowed the comment on the groceries to pass. He decided if Amy did the cooking, he'd supply the food.

"Mr. Matt." Rose chewed with her mouth open. "How did you know we liked Silly Nilly's?"

He didn't dare confess he'd stood in the cereal aisle for five minutes before he'd gathered the courage to ask a female shopper to suggest a treat for little girls. He shrugged. "You two look like Silly Nilly girls." Rose giggled and made a funny face. Lily mimicked her sister, then banged her spoon on the tray.

"Quit, Rose, or you'll have Lily all worked up and she won't eat." Amy passed the warm tortillas to Matt.

"Thanks for making supper." He loaded his plate with food. He'd skipped lunch, wanting to get to work cleaning the barn.

"How did things go today?" Amy asked.

"Good. I scrubbed the stall." Matt had disinfected everything that the stallion came in contact with including the cement floor. He wanted the animal to smell *him* and nothing else in the barn.

"Is SOS eating?" Amy's gaze dropped to her plate. He had a hunch her financial situation had forced her to scale back on feed for the stallion.

"Ate everything in sight today." Matt had stocked up on carrots and sugar cubes to reward SOS for good behavior.

This afternoon he'd set a piece of carrot on the stall door and stood nearby, assuming the animal would be wary of approaching the treat. Surprisingly the stallion hadn't balked at snatching the carrot from the top of the gate with Matt close by—which didn't make any sense if the horse had been mistreated. At that moment, with SOS munching in Matt's ear, he'd suspected Ben's death had been an accident. His gut said something or someone had set the horse off. But what?

After SOS had eaten the carrot, Matt had decided to examine the animal's hide for wounds or scars that might signal abuse, but when he'd opened the stall door the stallion had gone loco. SOS had danced sideways, stomped and swung his head from side to side. As soon as the stall door closed, the stud had quieted. Darndest thing Matt had ever witnessed.

"Rose, tell Mr. Matt what the rule is about the barn," Amy said.

"Lily and I can't go into the barn." The girl sighed dramatically. "Ever."

Although Amy put on a brave face, fear darkened her eyes. He understood and sympathized. She had a right to worry about the girls' safety. Whether accidental or not, she'd lost her husband to a violent death and was determined the girls wouldn't suffer a similar fate.

"That's a good rule, Rose. I bet you help your mom by keeping tabs on Lily and making sure she doesn't wander close to the barn."

"Rose is a big help around the farm." Amy smiled, sweeping the bangs off the girl's forehead.

The maternal gesture reminded Matt that his mother had left him and his sister when they'd been toddlers. He'd grown up with his father's love and had basked in the attention of Juanita, their housekeeper, but by the time his father had remarried, Matt had reached his teens and hadn't wanted a mother hovering over him.

"I done!" Lily announced.

"Yuck." Rose pointed to her sister's high chair.

The tray was smeared with mashed bits of food. Hardly any of the rice, beans or shredded tortilla pieces had made it into Lily's mouth. Food stuck to her hair, eyelashes, ears and Matt spotted a grain of rice protruding from her nose.

"I don't understand why she refuses to use her spoon." Amy blew out an exasperated breath.

Rose grinned at her sister. "Lily's a pig."

The word *pig* triggered a snort from the toddler and the speck of rice shot from her nostril like a pellet from a BB gun, hitting Matt in the chin.

"Sorry." Amy sprang from her seat, wet a dishcloth and attempted to wipe her daughter's face—not an easy task with the two girls engaged in a pig-snorting contest. Amy gave up, tossed the towel into the sink and ignored the ruckus while she ate.

Matt was content to sit on the sidelines and observe the three females. Amy's habit of taking a deep breath after every bite drew Matt's attention to her bosom, which she had plenty of for a small gal. He tended to gravitate toward tall, leggy redheads, not short, curvy blondes. But Amy's womanly softness snagged his interest.

"Are you finished?" Amy asked.

Had she caught him ogling? Matt tore his eyes from the front of her shirt. She nodded to his empty plate. "I'll warm up more tortillas—"

"No, thanks. I'm full. The food was great." Actually the meat was a bit on the tough side and made him wish for Juanita's cooking. He scanned the kitchen.

The room looked as if a food bomb had exploded inside it.

Pots and pans stacked in the sink. Dirty dishes and utensils scattered across the counter top. Food on the floor around the high chair. Leftovers waiting to be stored in the fridge. He eyeballed the door, contemplating a quick escape. Then he caught Amy rubbing her temples. Tired or upset? Probably both. The bank manager's visit had been a low blow. Then she'd slaved over a meal. And now she was faced with a massive cleanup and a dirty kid. Was it any wonder she was at her wit's end?

"Rose and I will tackle the kitchen if you want to give Miss Lily a bath," he offered.

She crinkled her nose. "What did you say?"

"I'm not much of a cook, but I'm a whiz at washing dishes." He'd noted the absence of a dishwasher among the kitchen appliances.

"You're sure?" she hedged as if fearing he'd rescind the offer.

"Positive. Go ahead and get the little one cleaned up."

Eyes glistening, Amy choked, "That would be great. Thank you." Then she cleared her throat. "Rose, you help Mr. Matt. Show him where things go." Amy lifted the grubby toddler from the high chair, and Lily shoved her sticky fingers right into her mother's curls before pressing a slobbery kiss to her cheek.

As soon as Amy left the room with Lily, Rose announced, "My daddy never washed dishes."

"Guess I'm a sucker for damsels in distress."

Chapter Four

Friday morning Amy stood in the kitchen, phone to her ear, attempting to convince her neighbor that Matt Cartwright was harmless. A week had come and gone and Matt had yet to work with SOS long enough to determine if the stallion was safe. Neither he nor Amy had brought up the agreement Matt had struck with her... "If the stud remains untouchable, I'll load up my mares and retreat to Oklahoma." Matt was determined to win over the horse and for reasons she refused to delve into, Amy was determined to let him.

"Mary, Matt Cartwright is on the up-and-up," Amy assured for the umpteenth time. Not once had he stepped out, over or under the line with her or the girls.

More importantly, he'd kept his promise. This past Monday he'd stopped at the bank in town and paid her May mortgage along with the late fees Payton had tacked on. She intended to pay back every penny as soon as she landed a job and saved enough for the upcoming June payment.

"Phone Jake Taylor," Amy said. "He's been checking in with Matt. He'll attest to the man's reputation."

Amy's neighbor droned on about how people couldn't be too careful these days—a drawback to living in a small community. Folks tended to be overly suspicious of outsiders—often for no good reason. Amy searched for the words to persuade the woman to allow her daughter to babysit the girls.

Her data class began Monday. Amy had hoped Mary's fifteen-year-old daughter would ride the school bus home with Rose each day, then watch the girls until eight in the evening when Amy returned from class.

"Mary—" Amy interrupted the woman's ramblings. "Would you allow Kristen to babysit if I arrange for Mr. Cartwright to be absent from the farm while she's here?" Amy had no idea how she'd convince Matt to leave the premises for five hours a day. Mary agreed to discuss the situation with her husband and call later that evening. Amy thanked her, then hung up. "Darn it!"

"Trouble?"

She spun and spotted Jake Taylor standing on her porch. "C'mon in, Jake."

He stepped into the kitchen. "Where're the little fillies?"

"Napping. Rose caught Lily's cold, so after school I made them both rest."

"Can I help?" Jake nodded at the telephone.

"I wish." She grabbed a mug from the cupboard and filled it with coffee. "Have a seat." Jake was a coffee-guzzling cowboy and his wife, bless her heart, hadn't brewed a decent pot of java their entire marriage. But Jake loved Helen as if there were no tomorrow and relied on sympathetic neighbors to satisfy his coffee urges.

"That was Mary Hainestock. I'm trying to convince her that Matt isn't a mass murderer so she'll allow Kristen to babysit the girls for the next few weeks while I take a data-entry course in Rockton."

Jake sipped from the coffee mug, then sighed his pleasure.

"I said you'd vouch for Matt," Amy continued. "But I suspect Mary won't call you."

"Did a little diggin' into Cartwright's background."

"Really?" She leaned forward. "What did you learn?"

"Spoke with a few buddies of mine who follow the rodeo circuit. Cartwright's one of the top tie-down ropers in the country."

"I noticed his buckle the other day," she confessed.

"He went to college while ridin' the circuit, too."

College? The cowboys she'd met had never gone to college—including Ben.

"Graduated with a business degree from Oklahoma State, then headed off to rodeo full-time." Jake shoved a bent finger under the brim of his hat and scratched the patch of thinning hair at the front of his head. When that same finger picked at the glob of dried spaghetti sauce on the kitchen table, Amy became suspicious.

"Spit it out, Jake."

"Cartwright's loaded."

Amy rolled her eyes. "Everyone's got money compared to me." She wasn't surprised by the information. It all added up—the fancy rig. The nice diesel truck. A real Stetson, not a knockoff. The fact he'd made her mortgage payment without batting an eye.

"His daddy does oil," Jake said.

"Oil like in…"

"Millions of dollars worth of oil wells in Oklahoma and eastern Arkansas."

Why in the world was Matt messing around with a deranged horse when he had enough money to purchase an entire stud farm? "Doesn't make sense."

"I figure the man's got his reasons for wantin' to work with SOS," Jake answered as if reading her mind. "Cartwright thinks the horse spooked when he kicked Ben."

She admitted that it was entirely possible her husband's death had been accidental, but that didn't make it any easier to accept.

"In any regard, the cowboy knows what he's doin' with the animal."

If Matt proved SOS wasn't loco she'd sell the animal and pay off most, if not all, her debt. Both her father and Ben had been big talkers. Talk didn't prove anything. Time would tell if Matt had the ability to rehabilitate the stud.

But Matt will never have the chance if you force him to leave the farm while Kristen babysits.

"Cartwright's a straightforward cowboy," Jake continued. "Never been married. No kids."

No kids that he's aware of... She scolded herself for the uncharitable thought. Just because the man was a walking, breathing hunk didn't mean he was reckless in bed. She squirmed in the chair, resisting the urge to ask if Matt was currently involved with a woman—not that she cared one way or another. *Yeah, right.* She blamed her horny musings on the dry spell her love life had suffered from since before Ben's death.

"Does Matt have the right equipment to work with

SOS?" She should have offered Matt a tour of the barn and shown him where the equipment and supplies were—what few remained.

Jake nodded. "Matt's got SOS in the paddock now. Prancin' around like he ain't kicked nobody."

Enough talk about horses and Matt. "How's Helen?" Jake's wife suffered from lupus and had her good days and bad days.

"Doc prescribed a new medicine. She's feelin' good enough to cook."

Helen came from a long line of Germans and was happiest slaving over a hot stove making Jake's favorite—sauerkraut and sausage. Amy didn't like cooking. She'd rather be outside with the horses or digging in her flowerbed. In her opinion the whole Betty Crocker thing was overrated. What pleasure did a woman gain from spending hours preparing a meal that would be devoured in a matter of minutes? Then the husband would head out to the barn and leave his wife to deal with a sinkful of dirty dishes.

"I'll stop by and visit Helen soon." Amy felt guilty for avoiding the older woman, especially when Helen loved seeing the girls. Since Ben's death Amy's life had become a toy top—spinning aimlessly in a world that shrunk inch by inch.

"Appreciate the coffee. Best be on my way." Jake carried his empty mug to the sink.

She followed him to the door. "Thanks for watching over us."

"Your granddaddy would have... Hold up." He patted his jean pocket, then removed a black notepad the size of an address book. "Almost forgot why I'd stopped by." He held out the pad. "I'm ashamed to admit I'm just now gettin' around to strippin' the paint off that old desk you sold me after your folks passed on. Found this book stuck between two drawers."

"It's my father's," Amy murmured, fanning the pages. "He carried it everywhere with him." She smiled at the memory. "He'd write ideas or sketch pictures of inventions he believed would make him rich one day." Amy had wondered where the journal had disappeared to. She hadn't seen it when she'd sorted through her parents' possessions after their deaths.

"Well, holler if you come across a winner. I wouldn't mind earnin' a few extra bucks before I die." He winked.

"You'll be the first to know if I discover a money-making scheme worth consideration." Amy hugged the geezer.

"Give Cartwright half a chance, young lady. If he can prove the stud was spooked and didn't attack Ben, SOS will fetch a good price."

Strange how the horse that killed her husband might be the means to a brighter future for Amy and the girls. One thing for certain, she was tired of being beholden to people. Whether she liked it or not, she needed Matt's help with the stallion.

As soon as Jake's truck pulled away, Amy shoved her father's notebook into a kitchen drawer—she'd read it later when she was in a better mood—and headed for the barn. Only the fear that if she didn't acquire a decent-paying job, she and the girls might end up homeless kept her from chickening out. But how did she tell Matt that he had to get lost for a few hours each day while she attended classes—especially after he'd shelled out sixteen hundred dollars for her mortgage payment?

"I was on my way up to the house." Matt flashed a white smile when he met her at the barn door. "How would you and the girls like to go out for supper tonight?"

Was he asking her on a date?

"It's Friday," Matt continued, unfazed by her silence. "Figured you'd want to get away from the place."

So he'd noticed that she and the girls hadn't left the farm this week—save for Rose, who hopped on the school bus each morning at seven-thirty. Lord, she led a pathetic life. "I'd planned to make—"

"You cooked all week. Let me treat you and the girls to a nice meal." His grin widened and the air in Amy's lungs escaped in a whoosh.

Yes, she'd prepared the meals, but he'd paid for the food. Then a terrible notion struck her. "You're not keen on my cooking, are you?"

If his smile widened any farther his lips would split in half. "Your meals are great, Amy."

Right. That must be why the giant-size ketchup bottle in the fridge was almost empty. "I appreciate the offer, but the girls and I will be fine right here." She rushed on. "Bailey's is a tavern in Rockton that offers a fish fry on Fridays. And the Cantina has decent Mexican cuisine— not real spicy." And her favorite... "DaVinci's has to-die-for fried ravioli." Her mouth watered, imagining the taste.

"Do the girls like Italian?"

"Well, sure they do, but—"

Eyes sparking he coaxed, "C'mon, Amy. Have dinner with me tonight." Then he inched forward and his scent almost overwhelmed her. He smelled of barn, faded cologne and the bar of Coast soap in her shower. For a few moments she forgot where they were. Forgot she was a widow. Forgot she had two children. Forgot everything but the sight, smell and yes, touch—she dropped her gaze to where his fingers toyed with hers—of this man.

"The girls will have fun," he insisted.

"The girls have colds." Why did her voice sound far away?

"Bring sweaters for them to wear in the restaurant."

Why would a cowboy like Matt want to hang out with a widow and two kids—because he was being nice or because he wished to please her so she wouldn't send him packing? As if either reason mattered because she was dying to escape the farm. "We'll pay for our own meals."

"No, ma'am. My treat."

Pride reared its ugly head. "I don't appreciate people feeling sorry for me."

"Is that what you believe—that I pity you?"

Eyes stinging, she admitted, "Maybe."

"I don't."

The note of conviction in his voice broke through her defenses. "All right, then. The girls and I accept your invitation."

"Be ready by five-thirty." He winked, then retreated deeper into the barn to finish whatever he'd been doing before she'd interrupted him.

Heart racing, she hurried to the house—what to wear out to dinner taking precedence over asking Matt to vacate the ranch when the babysitter arrived next week.

WHILE AMY PUTTERED IN the kitchen, Matt sat on the porch swing, battling a bad case of nerves. After they'd returned from the restaurant in Rockton, she'd put the girls to bed, then promised him coffee before he turned in for the night.

His dining experience with the three females had gone better than he'd anticipated. As Amy promised, the food at DaVinci's had been excellent. But after a bite or two the flavor was forgotten as he lost himself in watching Amy. She'd cut each piece of fried ravioli in half, then closed her eyes when she chewed, savoring the mouthful. He wondered if Amy made love the same way she ate—slow and easy. The pleasure on her face after swallowing had been sexier than all get out.

Afraid if he didn't quit thinking about Amy, food and sex he'd embarrass himself when they stood up to leave the restaurant, Matt had offered to teach Rose how to twirl spaghetti using a fork and spoon. As the meal progressed, the conversation had centered on the girls. Rose was a talker. Her favorite topic—her latest love, Butch. And Lily with her sweet smile and copycat words gathered her share of attention from the waitress.

He wished Amy would hurry with the coffee. After witnessing her lush lips chew food, he wanted to kiss her. Taste her. Test the softness of her lips. Maybe flick his tongue inside her mouth and whisk it over her teeth. A friendly kiss—nothing more. A thanks-for-going-out-to-supper-with-me kiss.

The phone rang inside the house and Amy answered it. Her muted voice carried through the screen door, but he wasn't able to decipher much of the one-sided conversation. A minute later, she stepped onto the porch, carrying two coffee mugs.

"Everyone tucked in for the night?" he asked.

She moved toward the porch steps.

Oh, no, you don't. He patted the seat. "The stars here seem brighter than the ones in Oklahoma," he said, hoping to break the tension.

Amy intrigued Matt. The widow came with more baggage than an airline employee handled in a week, yet that didn't faze him. Each time he lost himself in Amy Olson's brown eyes, a feeling of *home* rushed through him. Her small spread nestled in the lush valley along the banks of the south fork of the Snake River filled his soul with contentment and peace.

But the peace was temporary. No matter how much he admired her farm or wished to get to know Amy better, he didn't dare lose his heart to the woman— because she'd trample it to death if she discovered how he'd used her husband.

Besides, he'd sworn off women after the stunt Kayla had pulled on him.

Amy's not Kayla. She wouldn't use you.

Maybe. Maybe not. Where women were concerned Matt's judgment sucked. He'd been sure Kayla had been the one. Never in his wildest dreams would he have imagined the woman and her ex had been plotting against him—Kayla would marry Matt, then turn around and seek a divorce and a substantial financial settlement.

You're no better than Kayla. You used Ben Olson's gambling addiction for your own gain—that's just as bad.

Amy handed him one of the mugs before taking a

seat on the swing, scooting as close to the armrest as possible. He didn't mind. He closed his eyes and inhaled the smell of coffee and Amy's citrus shampoo.

"Rose claims she's going to teach Butch how to twirl spaghetti now."

Matt smiled as he recalled Rose's spaghetti-stained mouth at the restaurant. "How are the girls coping with their father's death?"

"Fine. Ben wasn't around much. Once a month he'd show up and stay for a few days, then he'd take off again. The girls understood he was their father, but they preferred to tag along after me." Then she abruptly switched topics on Matt. "I noticed the rope burn on your palm." Amy motioned to his right hand. "What happened?"

The diagonal line of puckered flesh dissected his palm from wrist to index finger. "A souvenir from my first bull ride."

"Jake said you were a roper."

"My bull-riding career lasted all of one ride. My hand got caught in the rope and the bull dragged me around the arena like a rag doll. When I tried to loosen the rope, my other hand—the one without a glove— got caught. After that experience I decided I was better off on a horse."

"Ben was leery of bulls, too. He busted broncs."

Matt knew who the better cowboys were on the circuit and Ben's name had never shown up in the standings or any win columns.

Amy's next words confirmed her husband's lackluster career. "He was in love with the whole rodeo-cowboy image. He stayed with the sport after we married because it was an excuse to leave the farm." She shrugged as if it didn't matter, but Matt caught the underlying hurt in her voice.

"How did you and Ben hook up?"

"We met at a rodeo, of course. He caught my eye with his full-of-himself attitude and smile." She cast a sideways glance. "All you rodeo cowboys have great smiles."

Did that mean Matt's grin was special or like a thousand other cowboys—not so special?

"At twenty-one I was naive about men. I was flattered by Ben's interest and mistook it for—" she waved a hand in the air "—real caring. We had a one-night stand in a motel room and Ben was gone the next morning. I was okay with that." She expelled a loud sigh. "Relieved actually. One of those life lessons you learn to accept and then move on. I came home and three months later discovered I was pregnant with Rose."

In the early days of his career, Matt had had his share of one-night stands. He'd been damned lucky none of the young ladies had ended up pregnant. He'd always been careful, but accidents happened. "Ben should have used protection."

"We did. The second time."

"So you and Ben married."

"I informed him because he had a right to know he was going to be a father. I didn't expect him to offer marriage. When he did, I accepted—mainly for my mother's sake." A red hue swept across Amy's cheeks. "I followed in my mother's footsteps. She ended up pregnant with me and had to marry my father." She sipped her coffee before continuing. "After we got hitched, Ben moved a few things into my bedroom here at the house."

"You two didn't want a place of your own?"

"Ben invited me to tag along with him on the circuit, but living in a pop-up trailer didn't appeal to me. Besides, my mother would never have been able to handle the boarding business by herself."

"She had your father—"

"My father was useless. Mom and I handled the horses." Her finger tapped against the ceramic mug. "The farm belongs to my mother's side of the family. My father never had any real interest in seeing the place prosper. I was fine with staying behind and letting Ben run off to his rodeos. And I admit I was nervous about being a new mother and wanted my mom close by for support."

"What happened to your folks?"

"They died a few years ago in a boating accident. Ben came home more often after that and I stupidly believed he'd intended to help around the place. Lily was the result of that bad judgment call."

"Mind if I ask how the farm got into financial trouble?" Matt braced himself for the answer.

"Ben gambled. A year ago I discovered he'd taken cash advances on several credit cards. When I threatened divorce, he begged for a second chance and agreed to join Gamblers Anonymous. A part of me hoped he'd change—for the girls' sakes." She stared into space for a long time. "I was such a sucker."

"What happened?"

"He insisted we take out a second mortgage on the

farm to pay off the credit cards and I agreed. But instead of paying off the debt, Ben used the money to buy SOS. He promised that stud fees would more than pay off our bills." She expelled a shaky breath. "A month later he died."

Matt couldn't ignore that he'd played a part in Amy's misfortune. "You're in a tough spot, all right," he murmured. He should pay her mortgage for the rest of the summer—the least he could do after he'd lured Ben into a card game the man had no business taking part in.

If Matt had the savings, he'd buy SOS from Amy right now and solve both their dilemmas. He contemplated asking his father for a loan, but the old man hated horses and Matt doubted he'd sink a single penny of the Cartwright oil fortune into Matt's dream.

Probably best. The more you help out Amy the more she'll ask for.

No. Amy wasn't another Kayla and gut instinct insisted Amy would pay him back eventually.

That's what Kayla said when you offered to buy the new equipment for her beauty shop.

All along he'd believed Kayla when she'd claimed she'd wanted nothing to do with the Cartwright millions. She'd hoodwinked him. He'd stupidly set her up in business and paid off her bills while Kayla had been two-timing him with her ex-boyfriend.

"I have a game plan," Amy said, shifting toward Matt. Her feminine scent chased away the ugly memories of the past. "Beginning Monday, I'm taking a three-week data-entry course. When I finish, I intend to find a job."

"Why another job? Once you sell SOS—"

"Whether I sell the stud or euthanize him, I need a job that provides decent health coverage for me and the girls."

Matt admired Amy's sound thinking. She wasn't waiting around to be rescued, she was taking her family's future into her own hands.

"But I have a problem," she continued. "Two problems, actually."

Suspicious, he asked, "What are they?"

Eyes glues to her lap, she played with the hem of her blouse. "I don't have the money to make my June mortgage payment."

Told you so. "I'll take care of it."

Chin high, she said, "I'll reimburse you as soon as I land a job."

Maybe he was a fool, but he believed her. "And the second problem?"

"The babysitter's parents won't allow her to watch the girls while you're working on thc farm."

"Why not?"

"You're a stranger around here. Even though I vouched for you as did Jake Taylor, this is a small community and folks are distrustful of outsiders."

Reining in his frustration, Matt insisted, "I have to work with SOS day in and day out to prepare him for brccding my mares," he argued.

"I'm sorry, but taking the girls to class with me would be a disaster."

"This wasn't part of our deal." He considered towing his mares and the stallion back to the Lazy River for the summer, but then he'd have to contend with his father sticking his nose into Matt's business. "I'll speak with your babysitter's parents and assure them I'm no threat to their daughter."

"I offered as much. They said no."

Matt set his mug on the porch railing and stood. "I'm sorry, Amy. You'll have to make other arrangements for the girls, because I'm staying right here with SOS."

His statement rendered Amy speechless, so he headed to the barn, wondering how the hell his plans for a good-night kiss had gotten derailed.

Chapter Five

"Watcha doing?"

Standing on a stool in the middle of the tack room, pitchfork high above his head, Matt froze. "Watch out, Rose. There's a huge rat on the loose."

A sweat broke out across Matt's forehead. When he was a kid he'd gotten bit by a rat and had undergone a series of painful rabies shots without a mother's hand to hold. From that day forward he'd kept his distance from any animal remotely resembling a rat—mice, gerbils, ferrets…squirrels.

He pointed his weapon at the cot across the room. "Hop on the bed before it comes out again."

She obeyed, using the cot as a trampoline. Too caught up in his fear, Matt hadn't realized right away that Rose had broken the golden rule on the farm. "You're not supposed to be in the barn."

Ignoring the accusation, Rose asked, "How come you don't eat with us anymore?"

Matt had risen Saturday morning, fired up over Amy's demand that he leave the farm five hours a day. To his way of thinking she should wait to enroll in the training class until he left the ranch. "I had to run an errand in Rockton yesterday," he explained, feeling bad that his absence had troubled the little girl.

The errand had to do with Maria's Cantina and chicken enchiladas. Afterward, he'd strolled around town, wasting a couple of hours before returning to the farm and spending the remainder of the evening at the corral discussing his dilemma with SOS.

Lower lip jutting out, Rose said, "Mama saved you a plate, but you didn't come get it."

Amy had kept supper warm for him? No wonder she'd snubbed his greeting this morning when he'd gone up to the house to use the bathroom and grab a cup of coffee. A movement startled Matt and he jabbed the pitchfork toward the corner of the room. "Hah! Scat, you beast!"

The black monster's long skinny tail stuck out from beneath the workbench, then it spun, red eyes glowing ominously. Matt shivered at the idea of sleeping on a cot six inches above the floor while a rat crawled around.

"Wait!" Rose hopped off the mattress, dropped to her hands and knees and crawled toward the workbench.

"Hey!" Matt blocked her path with the pitchfork. "What are you doing?"

"That's Sophia. She's my friend."

"Friend? That's a rat, Rose. Get back before it bites you." He hated to see a sweet girl like Rose have to undergo the painful rabies treatment.

"Sophia's my pet." She cooed gibberish to the rodent, which didn't appear wary of humans. "I bet you thought I forgot about you, huh, Sophia?" Rose glanced at Matt. "Sometimes I bring scraps from the table for her."

Matt wondered if Amy knew about her daughter's *friend.*

"But then Daddy died and Mama made me stay out of the barn." Eyes trained on the rat, she promised, "Next time I'm gonna bring you some cheese." When Rose stood, the rat scurried from sight. "Aren't you gonna get down?"

God, he wanted to. "I will as soon as I'm sure Sophia is gone."

"She won't hurt you."

"I'm not taking any chances." Why the heck was he arguing with a seven-year-old?

"Are you gonna stab her when I leave?"

The question evoked a gross picture in Matt's head. He supposed he'd have to buy a live trap or he'd be the world's cruelest cowboy if he killed the animal. "No. I'm trying to scare her so she keeps out of my way."

"She's lonely."

Rats don't get lonely. Matt scanned the floor one more time, then jumped off the stool. His heartbeat slowed to normal, but he refused to relinquish the pitchfork.

Now that the rat was no longer a threat, it was time to take Rose to task for entering the barn. "I'd better not catch you in here again, understand, young lady?" Most of the time SOS stayed in the paddock, but Matt hated to take a chance that one of the girls would wander through the barn when the stud was in his stall.

Hands on her hips, Rose pouted. "Are you gonna tell Mama?"

"No. You're going to tell your mother you broke the rule."

She stamped her foot. "Then I'm gonna tell Mama you're a fraidy cat."

Huh?

"And I'm gonna tell all my friends at school that you're scared of a—" she pinched her forefinger and thumb together "—a teeny, weeny little mouse."

"Sophia's a five-pound rat!" he protested.

Crossing her arms over her skinny chest, she said, "So?"

Darn, the little twerp had him over a barrel. He was tempted to call the girl a liar, but that would be mean. "Fine. You don't tell anyone I'm afraid of rats and I won't tell your mother that you snuck into the barn."

Rose's mouth stretched into a wide smile. "Thanks, Mr. Matt."

"But there's a catch," he added. "You have to promise never to enter the barn again by yourself."

"But who's gonna feed Sophia?"

"I will." He'd love to offer the rodent a handful of poison pellets, but wouldn't. Once he trapped the thing he'd release it somewhere far away—like Montana.

"Promise?" Rose begged.

"Yes." He nodded to the doorway. "How do you plan to leave the barn without your mother seeing?"

Slim shoulders shrugged.

He held out his hand and she took it. His grip swallowed her tiny fingers and he automatically loosened his hold. "C'mon."

At the barn door he peered out, making a big deal of surveying the yard. "Coast is clear." Then the squeak of the porch door caught Matt by surprise and he tugged Rose into the shadows.

"Rose! Rose, where are you?"

"Your mom's heading this way," he warned.

"I'm busted." The hangdog expression on the kid's face was the most pathetic sight he'd seen in ages. She squeezed his hand. "Don't worry, Mr. Matt. I'll still keep your secret."

"Stay here," he whispered, then stepped into the light. "Anything wrong, Amy?"

"Have you seen Rose? I told her to take the garbage to the compost pile."

"She headed inside a few minutes ago," he lied.

"We must have missed each other." Amy's gaze leapt around, refusing to settle on him. He wished she'd make eye contact—staring into her brown eyes gave him a warm, cozy feeling.

"Well." She scuffed the toe of her boot in the dirt. "I'd better make lunch." Finally she lifted her head and Matt felt as if he'd been sucked inside a vat of warm, sweet chocolate. His stomach growled loudly.

"You haven't come up to the house for a meal." The words were innocent enough, save for the accusatory note in her voice.

"Yeah, I'm sorry." He'd avoided the house and Amy for the past two days because he'd feared they'd get into another argument over her demand that he leave the farm when the babysitter arrived tomorrow—which he refused to do.

"Are you planning to eat lunch with us?"

"Ah…"

He must have hesitated too long, because she offered, "I'll leave a couple of sandwiches in the fridge."

"Thanks." Good thing Rose was crouched behind a

hay bale six feet away or he'd have brushed aside the damp curl clinging to Amy's cheek.

"I'd better see about finding my daughter," she said.

As soon as Amy vanished from sight, Matt pulled Rose from the shadows. "Run like the wind, kid."

"Thanks, Mr. Matt. You're the best."

Matt didn't feel like the best as he watched Rose sprint across the gravel drive. Amy made him feel like the rat hiding in the barn—a nuisance.

MONDAY MORNING USHERED IN the first week of June. Matt was grumpy. He'd slept in snatches, haunted by nightmares of giant rats cornering him in the barn. At 5:00 a.m. he'd rolled off the cot and dressed, then headed out to check on SOS and the mares. Yesterday had been the first time he'd left the stallion outside all night. He hadn't wanted to leave the stud in his stall in case Rose snuck back into the barn to check on Sophia.

Being confined in his stall made SOS nervous and Matt had yet to figure out why. He stopped at the corral and clucked his tongue. The stallion whinnied, then trotted closer. Matt offered a sugar cube, which the horse licked off of Matt's hand like a gentleman. Their good-morning ritual over, Matt spent a half hour shoveling the dung in the corral. Next he fed and watered the animals before grooming the mares and inspecting them for signs they were coming into season—nothing yet.

Today after SOS ate, Matt had plans to saddle the animal, but right now the stud was more interested in watching Chloe, the feistier of the three mares. Chloe charged the fence separating the two paddocks—as if saying, "come and get me." SOS played his own hard-to-get game. He snorted, then pranced off, pretending he wasn't interested in any of the mares.

Matt swung himself onto the top rail and enjoyed the show and the sunrise. He'd regarded Oklahoma sunrises as the prettiest in the country, but admitted the pink light bleeding over the farm's lush green hills dotted with gnarly oaks was an impressive sight. Amy's place was a good mile off the county road and only the sounds of chirping birds and whinnying horses filled his ears.

He'd come up with a plan to stay out of the babysitter's way when she arrived later in the afternoon and hoped Amy would agree to it. After several minutes he hopped down and headed to the house. He knocked on the door. No one answered, so he let himself in. The pitter-patter of little feet echoed upstairs as Amy got Rose ready for school.

After starting a pot of coffee, Matt helped himself to a bowl of Wheaties. Halfway through his breakfast, Lily, with her blond curls sticking up in every direction, shuffled into the room, clutching a pink blanket and sucking her thumb. She paused next to Matt's chair and studied him with her mother's big brown eyes.

"Mornin', Lily," he said.

The thumb popped out. "Mornin'," she mimicked, then popped the thumb back into her mouth.

"Ready for breakfast?"

The toddler moved to her high chair and waited to be hoisted up. Matt attempted to loosen the tray, but the task was beyond his cowboy capabilities. Admitting defeat, he laid the chair flat on the floor and slid Lily in feetfirst, then righted the seat. Her blanket was in the way of the safety buckle, so he grabbed it—*big mistake*. The kid let out a wail that threatened to wake her dead relatives sleeping up the hill.

Matt improvised by flinging the blanket over Lily's head, then snapping the buckle closed. When he went to tug the blanket off her, Lily shouted, "No!"

Now what? He knew zilch about two-year-olds. Did you offer them a choice of foods for breakfast or dump the cereal on the tray? "What do you want to eat, Lily?"

A muffled "Churos" answered back.

"Cheerios I can do, kid." He retrieved the cereal box from the pantry and poured a pile on the tray. Then he found the pink cup with the lid he'd seen the little girl use at mealtimes and filled it with milk. When Lily tugged the blanket off her head, her hair crackled with electricity. "Dig in." He shoveled a spoonful of soggy Wheaties into his mouth.

The toddler frowned, her eyes shifting to Matt, then to the cereal. "You have to stop sucking your thumb to eat, Lily."

She sucked the digit harder. Amy's voice—her sharp tone signaling that Rose wasn't cooperating—carried into the kitchen. "Sounds like Mommy's in a baaad mood, kiddo. I'd eat if I were you."

The threat went unheeded. The little twerp's cheeks continued to puff in and out as she sucked her thumb and rubbed the corner of the blanket against her nose.

Matt stared.

Lily stared.

They were at an impasse.

Amused by the child's stubbornness, he picked up a Cheerio from the tray and aimed it at her mouth.

"Catch," he said. The cereal ricocheted off her nose and her eyes crossed. "Strike one," he muttered, picking up another Cheerio. "Catch." This time the oat ring pinged off her forehead. The kid's lips twitched.

"Try to catch the Cheerio in your mouth." Matt missed her mouth and the Cheerio landed in her hair. Lily giggled.

He got caught up in the game and began firing Cheerios in quick succession, which earned him a belly laugh from Lily. When her thumb slid out of her mouth, Matt landed a piece of cereal on her tongue. Lily's eyes rounded, then she closed her mouth and chewed. As soon as she swallowed, she said, "Again," and opened her mouth.

Matt praised her while he tossed Cheerios. She'd finished half the cereal on the tray when Amy waltzed into the room. Her stunned gaze switched between Matt and her daughter, who had Cheerios stuck in her hair. "What are you doing? She's not a dog you throw treats to."

"I wanna play." Rose climbed onto the chair across from Matt, leaned over the table and opened her mouth.

"Rose, stop. You know better. Obviously Mr. Cartwright does not."

They were back to *Mr. Cartwright* again? "Sorry," Matt muttered, wondering if Amy intended to spank him—now that had possibilities. He admired her backside as she popped a waffle into the toaster. She must have sensed his scrutiny because she glanced over her shoulder and caught him focusing on her fanny. Despite the pretty blush suffusing her cheeks, her eyes flashed a warning. He grinned. "No harm in looking."

"Looking at what, Mr. Matt?" Rose asked.

Your mother's enticing derrière.

"Never mind. Rose, fetch the syrup bottle." Amy waltzed past the high chair and snatched Lily's blanket. Not a sound of protest from the pipsqueak. Mothers made everything seem easy.

"Eat fast, honey. The bus will be here in fifteen minutes." Amy stuffed a purple sparkled lunch box with an odd assortment of food, then filled the matching thermos with apple juice.

Realizing his talk with Amy would have to wait until Rose left for school, he relaxed in the chair and observed the girls' morning routine. "Do you like school, Rose?"

"It's okay. Reading time is fun."

"Reading is good." Matt often read while he traveled the circuit—mostly thrillers. He searched for another question. "Do you like riding the bus?"

"Yep. I sit next to Butch. He lets me read to him."

What kind of boy was this Butch? Matt wouldn't have been caught dead listening to a girl read to him. He watched Amy, noting the dark circles that rimmed her eyes. What had kept her up last night?

She glanced at the wall clock and frowned. "Would you mind driving Rose to the bus stop?"

"Yeah, Mr. Matt." Rose sat straighter in her chair. "You can see my bus."

"Bus!" Lily screamed and Matt jumped three inches off his seat.

Rose giggled and Lily joined in until Amy scolded, "Enough!" Then she said to her youngest, "Lily stays with Mommy."

Rose hopped off her chair. "We better go 'cause my sister's gonna cry."

He hadn't recalled agreeing to limo service, but didn't object when he saw Lily's cheeks glow tomato-red. The kid was about to blow a gasket. He held open the door. Rose hugged Amy, grabbed her lunch box off the counter and shot out of the house. With a last lingering glance at Amy, he left. The screen door hadn't even closed when Lily let loose a wail.

Matt lifted Rose into the front seat of his truck and hopped in after her. He drove the mile to the county road, then shifted into Park and shut off the engine while they waited for the bus. "You like country music?"

No answer.

"Listen to this." He popped in an oldies CD, and played "These Boots Are Made For Walkin'" by Nancy Sinatra. Matt's father must have played the song a million times after Matt's mother had left the family.

Matt sang along and Rose joined in after a bit. They were beboppin' in the seat and didn't notice the bus arrive until the driver laid on the horn. "It's here," Rose announced. Matt walked the little girl to the bus and flashed a smile at the female driver. "Mornin'."

"Bye, Mr. Matt." Rose waved, then found her seat.

"Tell Amy Rebecca says hello," the driver said.

"Will do." Matt wasn't sure what Amy did at this point, so he played it safe and waved as the bus drove off.

Feeling dumber than a jackass for having been caught goofing off with a seven-year-old, he made a U-turn in the truck and headed back to the house. On the way he switched the radio to a local weather station and was caught off guard by the prediction of a late-evening thunderstorm. Instead of working with SOS as he'd planned, he'd have to spend the morning preparing the barn stalls in case he had to bed down the horses for the night. By the time Matt parked the truck in the driveway he'd forgotten his intention to discuss the babysitter dilemma with Amy.

The hours passed quickly and once the barn had been cleaned and prepped, he hopped on Chloe and rode the property line, tightening sagging sections of fence that wouldn't hold against a strong wind.

It was two-thirty in the afternoon when he rode into the ranch yard and discovered Amy pacing the porch. When she spotted him, she scooped Lily off the bottom step and marched his way.

She wasn't smiling.

He removed Chloe's saddle and hung it over the paddock rail. After he let the mare loose inside and locked the gate, Amy shoved Lily into his arms.

"Whoa! What's going on?" The wiggling toddler bobbled in his arms.

"I'm going to be late," Amy said.

"Late for what?" He glanced at Lily, but she didn't have the answer, so he trailed after Amy.

"My class." She stopped at her truck. "I made a casserole for supper. Heat it at three-fifty for an hour." She hopped inside and shut the door, then called out the open window. "Lily's already had a nap. Don't let her sleep any more or she won't go to bed tonight. I left instructions on the table along with several neighbors' phone numbers in case of an emergency." She revved the engine. "Don't forget to pick up Rose at the bus stop at three!"

Mouth sagging, Matt watched the battered Ford drive off.

What the hell had just happened?

Chapter Six

Big chicken.

Amy sat in her truck, shoring up the nerve to enter her own home. After the way she'd shoved her daughters off on Matt earlier in the day she wouldn't blame the cowboy if he reined in his mares and hit the road tonight.

She prayed he wouldn't.

Today had been an emotional turning point for Amy. She'd been anxious about taking the data-entry class, but the professor had been encouraging and the eight other students like her—recovering from life's hard knocks—had been talkative and friendly. For the first time in months she'd chatted with people who hadn't stared at her with pity. She'd come away from the experience more confident and determined she'd be on her feet in no time at all.

But she couldn't do it alone. No matter how much it irked her to depend on someone—especially another cowboy—Amy needed Matt.

In order to complete the class and secure a job with health benefits she required his babysitting services.

And in order to sell SOS and use the money to pay off her debts, Matt had to prove the stud wasn't deranged. Once she sold the animal, she'd resume her boarding business. With two jobs and the credit cards almost paid off, she'd no longer be considered a financial risk and the bank wouldn't be able to touch her farm.

As much as she hated to admit it, her family's future on the Broken Wheel rested heavily on both her and Matt's shoulders.

Time to face the music. The prospect of confronting Matt, getting the girls ready for bed, cleaning up the messes left over from the day and then doing her homework dampened her newfound excitement, leaving her mentally and emotionally weary.

When she entered the kitchen, she froze. Save for Lily's pink sippy cup sitting in the dish drainer on the counter, the room was spotless. Amy set her canvas book bag on the table, then perused the contents of the refrigerator. The casserole was gone. *No leftovers?* Lily ate like a bird and Rose had a normal child's appetite so Matt must have devoured huge helpings to finish off the dish.

She spotted the notebook paper she'd written a to-do and not-to-do list on for Matt. A black checkmark appeared next to all ten items. He'd done what she'd asked. And more— she hadn't expected him to provide maid service.

The girls' laughter echoed from the second floor. What were they up to? Amy slipped off her shoes and left them by the door. The sound of splashing water met her ears when she reached the landing at the top of the stairs. Bath time hadn't been on the *to-do* list.

She tiptoed along the hallway, then spied through the crack in the partially open bathroom door. Lily and Rose splashed in the tub, up to their chins in bubbles, and Matt sat on the floor propped against the wall across from the tub, his long lean legs stretched out before him.

"Mr. Matt, Lily's got a new hairstyle." Rose rubbed bubbles into her sister's curls and pulled the strands into a ponytail that stuck up on the top of her head.

"You look gorgeous, Miss Lily."

"Yeah, Lily," Rose giggled. "You're gorgeous."

Then Rose smashed her sister's hair flat and Matt cautioned, "Not too rough or she'll slip under the water."

"Will you make me a new hairstyle, Mr. Matt?" Rose pleaded.

Wide-eyed, Amy slunk into the shadows, wondering what the cowboy would do. Darned if he didn't scoot forward, lean over the tub and style her daughter's hair.

While Matt shaped Rose's hair into two horns on her head, Amy's eyes strayed to his gluteus maximus. His butt filled out the faded denim to perfection. She envisioned his muscular thighs bracketing her body, holding her steady while he— *Oh. My. God.* She sucked in a quiet breath and forced the X-rated image from her mind. She had no business fantasizing about Matt Cartwright.

"All done," he mumbled.

"I wanna see," Rose demanded.

"Hang on." When he lifted her daughter out of the water, Amy noticed Rose was wearing a two-piece swimsuit. She wondered whose idea that was. He swung Rose over the edge of the tub and held her up in front of the mirror above the sink. "Cool!" Then he plopped her back into the tub.

"Aren't you gonna wash our hair and stuff?"

"Isn't that what the bubbles are for?" he said.

Rose shook her head, the movement collapsing one of her horns. "Mama washes our hair and she's gotta scrub Lily 'cause she's too little to reach all the spots."

"I've never cleaned spots on little girls before so I think that's something your mother should do." Matt retrieved a clean cloth from the cabinet next to the tub. "You wash your sister."

"Yuck!" Rose protested.

Time to intervene. Amy retreated to the top of the stairs, then called, "What's everybody doing?"

"Mama's home!" Rose shouted.

"Mama. Home!" Lily copycatted.

Amy entered the bathroom. "Wow, that's a lot of bubbles."

"Mr. Matt let us use his bubble bath," Rose explained.

"How nice of Mr. Matt." Amy snuck a glance at the cowboy and his blue-eyed gaze knocked her heart sideways. He didn't look any worse for wear after spending half a day chasing little girls. Stubble shadowed his chin and cheeks, adding a dangerous edge to his already sexy face. The one thing missing was his lethal smile and she accepted full blame for his sober face.

Slowly, Matt stood. His expression...not cold, but not warm, either. She deserved that and more. Swallowing hard she said, "Thanks for your help with the girls today."

"Guess you can take it from here."

He stepped past her, but paused in the doorway when Rose called, "'Night, Mr. Matt."

"'Night, Mer Matt."

"Sweet dreams, girls." Then he was gone.

Amy's ears tuned in to the sounds of his footfalls on the stairs and a minute later the slamming of the door. She was halfway to the window overlooking the gravel drive when Rose's pronouncement stopped her in her tracks.

"The water's getting cold, Mama."

Grabbing the shampoo bottle, Amy said, "We'd better hurry then." A half hour later, the girls were squeaky clean and dressed in their pajamas.

"Snack," Lily squealed.

Amy's apology would have to wait a while longer. "Head to the kitchen. I'll be right there." She returned to the bathroom and mopped up the puddles, then collected Rose's swimsuit, the wet towels, even Matt's brown one from the hook on the door. She buried her face in its damp softness and breathed in his scent—a combination of soap, shampoo and his shaving cream.

"Lily, give it back!" Rose's cry disrupted Amy's sniffing fantasy and she hurried downstairs.

After snacks, she transferred the bath towels from the washing machine to the dryer, then hustled the girls upstairs to use the potty and brush their teeth before tucking them into bed—Rose in the big-girl single bed and Lily in the toddler bed a few inches above the floor.

"How was school today?" she asked.

"Good." Rose's usual response.

"Any homework?"

"Spelling words, but Mr. Matt helped me learn 'em."

"He did?"

"Uh-huh."

"I hope you thanked him."

"Uh-huh."

Amy yearned to hear how Lily's afternoon had passed, but the pipsqueak didn't possess the vocabulary to explain. Focusing in class today had been difficult with her mind in a constant state of worry. Worry that Matt wasn't keeping an eye on the girls. Worry that the girls would go into the barn or wander too close to the corrals. Worry that Matt would leave the gas oven on after heating the casserole.

Because she no longer had cell phone service, she'd used the payphone during a break in class and had called the house, but no one had answered. She'd immediately phoned Jake Taylor and had asked him to stop by the farm. To be safe, she'd made another call to her neighbor Mary and begged the woman to drop by the house.

"How's Butch?" she asked her daughter.

Rose exhaled loudly. "Butch lost his recess."

"Again?" The boy had sat out of recess three times the previous week.

"He made bite marks on Winnie's crayons in art class."

"So who did you play with at recess?"

"Winnie. And Brittany. We stayed on the swings."

Should she ask or leave it alone? *Ask.* "How did the bus ride go this morning?" Not until after Matt and Rose had driven off did Amy realize what she'd done. Rebecca, the bus driver, had probably spread the word through the grapevine that Amy had a man staying at her place. A handsome, sexy, cowboy kind of man.

Nothing remained private in small towns. Pebble Creek was no exception. Neighbors and friends often acted surprised when they heard news about others, but chances were they'd known days prior.

"Did Miss Rebecca ask about Mr. Matt?"

"No. But she said he's…" Rose licked her finger, then stuck it in the air and hissed like a snake. "Hot."

Good grief. "You didn't repeat that to Mr. Matt, did you?"

Rose shook her head.

Lily set her picture book on the floor, then snuggled under her cover and stuck her thumb into her mouth. Amy had tried all sorts of tricks to coax her daughter to quit her thumb-sucking habit, but with no success. After Ben's death she didn't have the energy to fight the small battles anymore. "Did any of the neighbors stop by to say hello?" she whispered.

"Mr. and Mrs. Taylor did. Mrs. Taylor brought us cookies and we sat on the porch swing while Mr. Taylor helped Mr. Matt in the barn."

"Anyone else?" Amy prodded.

"Nope."

"Did the telephone ring?"

"Kristen's mama called and Mr. Matt talked to her."

"Anyone else?"

Rose shrugged.

So much for Mary's promise to visit the girls.

Amy kissed Rose's shiny forehead, then repeated the gesture with Lily, who had already succumbed to sleep. "'Night, sweethearts."

Before Amy flicked off the light, Rose asked, "Is Mr. Matt gonna watch us tomorrow, too?"

"We'll see."

"I like Mr. Matt. He didn't get mad when Lily peeded her pants."

Darn, Amy knew she'd forgotten to do something

before she left. She'd planned to put Lily in a pair of pull-ups. "What did he do with her wet underwear?"

"Soaked 'em in the sink."

"Which sink?"

"The kitchen," Rose answered.

Next on *her* to-do list was to disinfect the sink. "'Night-'night." She closed the door halfway, left the hall light on, then retreated to the kitchen. After scouring the sink with cleanser, she stuffed her feet into her barn boots and headed outside, praying for the right words to convince Matt to babysit the girls again tomorrow.

HERE SHE COMES.

Matt stood inside the barn, his eyes on the house. He had a hunch Amy would seek him out. And after spending several hours playing Mr. Mom, he had a few things to say to the woman. Until Amy Olson no one had ever bossed Matt around—except his father. The fact that Matt had let her worried him. When she'd shoved Lily into his arms earlier in the day and had driven off he'd been too stunned to protest and had stood there like a dope.

He'd yet to decide whether to admire Amy for having the guts to stick to her plans and leave her daughters with him or to believe she was a terrible mother for abandoning the girls with a stranger. Okay, he admitted he wasn't a stranger anymore, but he sure wasn't Uncle Matt. Then he'd stopped thinking about Amy period when Lily had begun crying, *"Mama, Mama,"* and wiggled like a monkey to escape his hold.

When a few shushes hadn't done the trick, Matt had hauled ass into the house and headed straight for the pantry. Once he shoved the Cheerios box at the kid, the crying slowed to an occasional hiccup. He'd put Lily in the high chair and poured a handful of cereal on the tray—that's when he'd noticed Amy's note. She'd listed ten things—three of which basically said the same thing: Don't take his eyes off the girls. Keep the girls away from the barn. And don't leave the girls alone in the house.

He'd read the instructions twice, but almost forgot to retrieve Rose from the bus stop. Carrying the car seat Amy had left on the porch in one hand and Lily plus the Cheerios box she refused to relinquish in the other, he'd headed to his truck. Installing the car seat took more time than saddling a horse. Once he'd buckled Lily in he'd sped along the gravel drive, worried he'd be late. He had been. The bus sat parked on the shoulder with Rose waiting by the driver's side. When Lily spotted her sister she'd screeched, "Ro," and Matt damn near drove into the ditch.

Overall the day had gone better with Rose home. The problem with the first-grader—and he had appreciated her help with Lily—had been the girl's constant criticism. *Mama does it this way. Mama does it that way.* Finally he'd told Rose that things were going to get done Mr. Matt's way and she'd better quit yapping at him.

The final straw had been suppertime. He'd read the baking directions Amy had taped to the top of the foil-covered dish in the fridge, then had peeked inside and groaned—noodles and spaghetti sauce. Ketchup wouldn't go with that. Rose had eaten the casserole, but Lily had mostly played with her food, so he supplemented her meal with additional Cheerios.

When the girls had gone out to play in the backyard, he'd dumped the rest of the casserole in the compost pile alongside the barn. On the way to the house it had occurred to him that he might have saved a helping for Amy, but he shrugged off the concern. At least he wouldn't be stuck with leftovers tomorrow.

Tomorrow. That was the crux of Matt's dilemma. If not for Jake Taylor and his wife stopping by before supper he'd never have been able to work with SOS today.

"Matt?" Amy called when she stepped inside the barn.

He moved from the shadows and she jumped, pressing her palm to her chest. His eyes settled on her hand...er, breast. He figured after Amy had left him high and dry today, he could get away with a heck of a lot more than leering if he dared to.

"Girls in bed?" he asked.

"Out like a light." She scuffed her boot against the cement floor. The scraping sound had the mares turning their heads in the stalls. "You brought the horses in?"

"A line of storms are headed this way later tonight."

"I didn't know." Then she explained, "The radio in my truck is busted. How severe is the weather expected to be?"

"Heavy rains and gusty winds."

"Will you be all right out here?"

"Storms don't bother me." He paused. "I don't appreciate having the girls dumped on me."

The pink color faded from her cheeks, leaving her skin pale. "I owe you an apology."

"I'd rather have an explanation."

"Kristen's parents refused to allow her to babysit."

"And you assumed I wouldn't mind filling in?"

"I knew you'd say *no* if I asked for your help."

"But you dropped them in my lap anyway."

She shoved a hand through her curls, making an even bigger mess of her hair. "I was desperate," she whispered.

He scoffed and she stamped her foot. Now Matt knew where Rose got her stubborn streak. He clamped his lips together to keep from grinning at the grown woman's tantrum.

"If I'm going to keep this farm, I can't simply board horses. I need a second job that provides a stable source of income."

"Well, your goal is interfering with mine."

An unladylike snort echoed through the barn, triggering a symphony of horse whinnies. "Jake claims you're filthy rich. You can afford to buy a hundred studs. Why not chalk up your thirty-thousand-dollar loss to my husband to experience, bad luck or fate and move on?"

Matt steeled himself against the wobble in her voice. "Let me clear up one thing—" in case Amy got the idea to swindle money out of him like Kayla had "—my father is filthy rich, not me. I pay my own way through life. Always have, always will. Second, I don't want *just* any stud for my mares. SOS comes from a long line of award-winning stock. Third, quit changing the subject." When she opened her mouth, he rushed on. "I am not babysitting the girls again, so you'd better make other arrangements."

Her teeth worried her lip. "Were they that much trouble?"

What did behaving or misbehaving have to do with his refusing to play nanny? "No more trouble than livestock, which have to be fed, watered and hosed down from time to time." He supposed it wouldn't hurt to admit... "Rose was a big help with Lily." That was as much as he'd say. He didn't want to give Amy the idea that he'd enjoyed spending time with her daughters even if he did find the pint-size females as amusing as they were exhausting.

The girls had worn him out—physically, emotionally and mentally. Following their thought processes, anticipating their every move and deciphering Lily's vocabulary had taken more energy than roping steers. For the first time he'd wondered if his mother had abandoned him and his sister because she hadn't been able to cope with the demands of motherhood. He wasn't making an excuse for his mother, but accepted that some women weren't cut out for child rearing.

"Rose said Jake and Helen stopped by."

"Jake helped me out in the barn for a while." Then Matt rushed to add, "His wife watched the girls."

"Are you making progress with SOS?" Her eyes flashed toward the stud's stall.

"Not as much as I'd hoped to today," he said, lest she forget what they'd been discussing—his refusal to watch the girls.

"Are you going to ask me about the class?" She offered a shy smile, determined to change the subject.

Shoving aside his irritation, he grumbled, "How

was your class?" He walked over to the hay bale he'd popped open in the corner.

Amy followed. "Eight students are taking the class, including me." She chuckled, the sound more sensuous than humorous, causing a zing of awareness to shoot through Matt's bloodstream. "I was surprised to discover I wasn't the oldest."

"How old are you?" he asked.

"Twenty-eight. Some days I feel like I'm forty."

He swept an appreciative glance over her body. "You don't look forty."

"Thanks. I think." Then she volleyed the question back to him. "How old are you?"

"Thirty-four."

"You don't look forty, either."

He grinned, finding it difficult to remain angry when she teased him. While he forked hay into the stalls, Amy chatted. Her words were lost on him as he concentrated on her voice—the melodiousness of it was a whole lot different from when she bossed the girls around. Did her moans and sighs sound as sweet when she was making love?

"Matt?"

"What?" He set the pitchfork aside.

"You haven't heard a single word I've said, have you?"

"Sorry," he muttered, brushing his shirtsleeve across his sweaty brow. He'd allowed Amy to chatter long enough. "Listen. Being your nanny wasn't part of the deal. If my time is cut short with SOS my mares won't become pregnant and you won't be able to sell the stud." He paused and swore under his breath. Tears? *Ah, damn.*

A drop of moisture escaped one of her chocolate-colored eyes, rolled alongside her nose then dipped into the corner of her mouth.

If he had a lick o' sense, he'd pack up his horses and mosey along. The last time he'd fallen for a woman in distress he'd been made a fool of. The idea that he might repeat the same mistake with Amy had Matt questioning his IQ.

She sniffed. "The class lasts three weeks."

Damn. His horse-breeding plans were about to take a backseat to helping the widow. "I'll give you one week to find a babysitter. But that's it. No more deals." *And no more tears.*

She flung herself at him, knocking the pitchfork from his hands. He caught her around the waist and stumbled, but managed to keep them from tumbling to the ground.

"Thankyouthankyouthankyou."

With her breasts flattened against his chest, and his nose buried in the soft curls bobbing around her head, Matt prayed for the strength to resist this woman. Then Amy tilted her head. Her cheek rubbed his whiskers. Her breath caressed his ear.

He froze.

She froze.

They locked eyes.

Matt wasn't sure who inched forward first—not that it mattered. Mouths touched. Rubbed. Opened. Soon he was lost in the sweet taste of Amy Olson.

Chapter Seven

Matt entered Pebble Creek Feed & Tack Tuesday morning with a plan he hoped would enable him to work with SOS in the corral while keeping an eye on the girls.

The store was spotless and smelled of lemon cleaner—a far cry from the mercantiles he'd strolled through over the years. The shelves were neatly organized, the items pulled forward to the edge. Bright blue signs hung from the ceiling advertising popular products. The register sat smack-dab in the center of the store.

"May I help you?"

Matt spun. A middle-aged man wearing jeans, a Western shirt and a bolo tie materialized out of thin air. He offered his hand. "Clifford Burns. My granddaddy opened the store in 1949."

"Matt Cartwright." After the handshake, he said, "Got a few things to pick up today. First on the list is soft fencing."

"Aisle six. What are you intending to keep in or out?" Clifford asked.

"Kids." At the man's frown, Matt rushed on, "Do you carry walkie-talkies?"

"Yes, sir." He pointed to the glass case in front of the register. "Got a pair of Motorola T8500 Talkabouts."

"I'll check them out." Matt glanced up at the signs. "Live traps?"

"What size animal?"

"A barn rat."

Clifford scratched the bald spot in the middle of his head. "You want to relocate a rat?"

"Yeah, it's a long story."

"Anything else?"

"A bell. Like those old-fashioned ones mothers rang to call the kids in at suppertime."

"That it?"

"For now."

"Traps are in the storeroom. Got a couple of bells over there." Clifford pointed to an aisle behind Matt. "Be back in a minute."

Once the store owner vanished, Matt browsed the fencing supplies. He settled on an orange barrier fence, then selected two rolls of the four feet by a hundred feet plastic mesh and several mounting posts. He carried the fencing to the register and noticed that Clifford had placed the walkie-talkies on the counter for Matt to examine. The two-way radios had a twenty-five-mile range and came with a weather alert system, rechargeable batteries and a carrying belt that went around the waist.

Clifford had yet to emerge from the stockroom with the trap so Matt hunted for the bell. He found two—the style reminding him of a miniature Liberty Bell. He carried the box to the counter and examined the contents, making sure the hardware to install the bell was included.

The squeaking front door alerted Matt that another customer had entered the store.

"Well, well. The widow's handyman."

Matt's shoulders tensed. He recognized the voice even before he turned—the weasel-headed banker.

Dressed in a suit and tie, Payton Scott strutted across the floor, eyeing the items on the counter. "What's all that for?"

None of your business. "I'd planned to stop by the bank with a check for Amy's June mortgage payment. Thanks for saving me the trouble." Matt pulled the draft he'd written earlier from his wallet and stuffed it inside Scott's suit pocket.

"You're delaying the inevitable. Amy's too far in the hole to dig herself out." The banker squinted. "You're not really staying at her place to work with that stallion, are you?"

"What are you talking about?"

"You want that farm for yourself," he accused.

"You're nuts, Scott." Or was he? Matt pretended interest in the walkie-talkies, but his mind raced. Amy Olson's farm was a prime piece of real estate. Fertile land for grazing, two wells and a creek that ran through the middle. He'd never find land like that in Oklahoma. "I don't want the Broken Wheel." Then he added, "You seem intent on causing Amy a lot of grief."

"The way I see it, we're both using Amy."

Matt didn't immediately respond. Was he using Amy? *No.* He was spending his own cash to feed the livestock, himself, Amy and the girls. He'd made a second mortgage payment for her. And if that wasn't enough he'd been trumped into playing babysitter for a week. To his way of thinking, Amy had the better end of the deal. Or did she?

Because of her husband's reckless disregard for his family's future, Amy had been left in a lurch when he'd died. She had no choice but to train for a job she didn't want to do in order to support herself and the girls. Matt admitted he'd never known that kind of insecurity and probably never would. When his father's oil wells ran dry and had to be capped, there would still be an endless supply of money invested in stocks, funds and various portfolios for generations to come.

Even if Amy managed to keep up with the mortgage and taxes there would be little or no money left to pay off her debts, unless she was able to sell SOS, and Matt was determined to make that possible. "Why are you harassing Amy? Thought all you small-town folk stuck together."

"Listen, big shot. I know who you are."

He'd guessed Scott would investigate him—probably the same afternoon he'd stopped by Amy's. "Then you should know I don't give small-town bankers the time of day."

"If that's true, what do you want with a small-town hussy like Amy?"

"Better watch how you speak about the lady."

"So it's that way between you two? Had Amy let on she was horny, I'd have volunteered to scratch her—"

Matt's fist connected with the banker's nose and the sound of crunching bone reverberated through the quiet store. Blood sprayed the front of Matt's shirt and dripped off Scott's chin.

"You broke my nose!" the banker wailed, stumbling sideways. He pinched his nostrils and glared.

Clifford burst from the storeroom, hauling a wire trap. "What happened?"

"What do you think, Cliff? Cartwright punched me."

"Want me to call Nathan?" Clifford's eyes swung between the two men.

Who the hell was Nathan?

As if the store owner read Matt's mind, he explained, "Nathan's the local veterinarian." Then he added, "The nearest medical clinic is forty miles away."

"I ought to call the sheriff and have him throw your carcass in jail."

Matt held out his cell phone. "Go ahead. I'm sure the sheriff would be interested in hearing how you slandered Amy."

Scott glared, his eyes narrowing to slits before stalking out the door.

Relieved to have the banker out of his hair, Matt apologized. "Sorry for the disturbance. I don't make a habit of punching people, but Scott had it coming." When Clifford's expression remained tight, Matt decided to end the chitchat. "What do I owe you for this?"

After he loaded his purchases into the truck, Matt was too agitated by his tussle with the banker to return to the farm. Instead, he headed to Pearl's, hoping a strong cup of coffee would settle his nerves.

When he entered the café, he noticed a few stragglers remained from the breakfast rush. "Kind of early for lunch, ain't it?" Pearl called out.

"Time to refuel." Matt slid onto a stool at the counter. "Give me a cup of leaded, would you?"

"Gottcha covered, cowboy." Pearl grabbed a white ceramic cup from beneath the counter, snagged the coffeepot from the warming plate and poured. "Who's DNA you wearing on the front of your shirt?"

"Payton Scott's." He flexed his right hand and winced. Pearl caught the movement and retreated to the kitchen. A minute later she placed a baggie of crushed ice across his knuckles.

"Thanks, Pearl."

"Anyone who smacks Payton Scott upside the head is a hero in my book." In no hurry to top off the other patrons' cups, she said, "Payton ain't much of a fighter. He's a talker."

"Yep. Shooting off at the mouth is what did him in."

Resting her forearms on the counter, Pearl smacked her gum. "What'd the sissy pot say?"

Gossip. Matt detested hearsay—he'd been the recipient of his fair share most of his life. But if he didn't speak up first, Scott would likely stretch the truth and make himself out to be the good guy. "He insulted Amy's character and insinuated that I'm sleeping with her."

Pearl's jaw dropped, then a moment later she snapped it shut. "Ain't none of Payton's beeswax, who Amy sleeps with. But the girl's got a screw loose if she's shut the bedroom door in *your* face."

Because he was a rodeo cowboy most women believed all he was after was a wham-bam-thank-you-ma'am. That's why he'd been taken in by Kayla. Kayla had played hard-to-get. Not until it was too late and he'd lost his heart to the woman had he discovered that her *good-girl* role had been an act.

"Amy and I are not having an affair." Matt wasn't certain who he was trying to convince, the café owner or himself. He and Amy might not have had sex, but he'd sure as heck fantasized about mattress dancing with her after the kiss they'd shared yesterday.

Her mouth had set his lips on fire. He hadn't expected the mother of two to use her tongue in such wicked ways. She'd left him with a big ol' ache in his groin when she'd walked out of the barn. He'd gone to bed too preoccupied reliving their kiss to worry whether Sophie came out of hiding and bit him.

The woman tied Matt in knots. He admitted he was surprised that he was attracted to her. She wasn't knock-a-man-off-his-feet gorgeous. Or take-your-breath-away stunning. She was Amy. Her beauty was soft and subtle. A man had to study her face to see its charm and sweetness. And if he cared enough to gaze deep into her eyes, he'd notice the ordinary brown color changed with her moods—lighter when she laughed or smiled. Darker when she scowled. And almost black when she fretted.

Until Amy, he hadn't known *subtle* to be sexy.

Matt feared all Amy had to do was crook her finger and he'd come running. He'd awoken this morning thankful at having been saddled with Rose and Lily the remainder of the week. Their little faces reminded him that Amy had too much baggage attached to her—the girls, a dead husband and a defunct horse-boarding business. Kayla had had baggage, too. She hadn't bothered to mention her son or her struggling hair salon until after he'd fallen in love with her. He might have forgiven her if not for having discovered her ex-boyfriend had been warming Kayla's bed when Matt had been on the road. Greed made people do inexcusable things.

"Once my mares conceive I'm heading home to Oklahoma," he told Pearl. He snatched the menu from between the ketchup bottle and sugar shaker and refreshed his memory on the café's offerings. "I'll take two orders of macaroni-and-cheese with franks and a Rueben sandwich." Then he added, "To go, please."

Pearl opened her mouth to comment, but a customer called her name and she walked off without a word. The bell above the café door clanged and Matt recognized the customer.

Jake helped himself to the stool next to Matt. "Thought I spotted your rig in the lot."

"What's up, Jake?"

"You watchin' the princesses again today?"

"Yep." Amy probably believed all she had to do now was kiss him to enlist his cooperation.

"Want me to stop by later with Helen?"

"Appreciate the offer, but I've got things under control." Pearl waltzed by, set a mug on the counter for Jake, filled it with coffee, then departed for the kitchen.

"Heard you had a run-in with Payton Scott at the feed store."

"I'm sure everyone in town knows by now." Matt wondered if he'd have a chance to explain what had happened to Amy before the news reached her.

"Judgin' by the condition of your shirt, looks like you got the best of him."

"Scott had a few words to say about Amy that I took exception to."

"Glad to hear that gal's got a man stickin' up for her."

Matt was saved from discussing his relationship with Amy when Pearl placed a carryout bag on the counter. "Here you go, cowboy."

"Thanks." He added a ten-dollar tip to the bill, hoping the money would persuade the waitress from blabbing his food order across the county line. He didn't want Amy discovering that he intended to feed the girls takeout tonight instead of another one of her casseroles.

"Take this with you." Pearl handed him a laminated menu, then called over her shoulder as she walked off. "We deliver."

Before Matt left, he asked Jake the one question that had been on his mind the past couple of days. "Do you have any idea why Payton Scott's so interested in Amy's farm?"

"I suspect 'cause it's prime horse property and wealthy folk from the city's always searchin' for a place in the country."

If Payton expected Amy to give up her farm without a fuss, the man was in for a big surprise. Whether Matt liked it or not, his fight with the banker proved Matt had done what he'd sworn not to—he'd become Amy's champion.

AMY STOOD IN FRONT OF the kitchen window—a habit that was becoming all too frequent since Matt had arrived at the farm. Lily was napping and Amy had already prepared a chicken-and-rice casserole for supper. She'd doubled the recipe, hoping there would be leftovers when she returned from class tonight.

At half-past noon she had two hours to blow before heading into Rockton. She should be tackling the laundry, vacuuming, mopping, scrubbing toilets—anything but admiring the way the noon sun reflected off Matt's naked torso.

The stallion's dark brown coat glistened with sweat as Matt paraded him around the corral with a lead rope. At each turn man and beast stopped. After a minute SOS would nudge his nose against Matt's shoulder and Matt would resume walking. Amy wasn't sure what purpose the exercise served, but she did notice that the horse acted more relaxed and at ease outside in the corral than he did in his barn stall.

She hoped the stud made enough progress so Matt could turn the horse loose with the mares. Amy yearned for Matt to hang around the farm the entire summer.

All because of a kiss.

Wow had been the first word that had popped into her brain after their lips had separated yesterday. His mouth, gentle and demanding at once, had left her wanting to feel the press of his lips against other parts of her body. Perspiration dotted her brow as she envisioned the lower half of his body sans clothing. She shook her head, hoping to dislodge the sensual daydream. She had no business contemplating a future with Matt—even a future measured in days or weeks. She'd lusted after a cowboy once and that had led to widowhood before her thirtieth birthday and in debt up to her ears. She'd learned the hard way that the only person she could depend on was herself.

But you depended on Matt to watch the girls and he didn't let you down.

True. Amy had never left the girls with Ben because he'd become preoccupied with his own activities and forget about Rose and Lily for long periods of time. She still worried over Matt watching the girls, but instinctively she knew her daughters would be safe with him. Amy didn't understand it, but in the short time since Matt had arrived at the farm, he'd come to earn her trust. His determination and hard work with SOS proved how serious he was about succeeding with the stallion. In the end if she wasn't able to sell the horse, Matt wasn't to be blamed. The man was no slacker.

Aside from both cowboys being handsome, Matt wasn't like Ben in any way, which made Matt all the more dangerous to Amy's heart. The temptation to throw herself at Matt was mighty, but she'd never be anything more to him than a summer fling. Besides, the cowboy could do better than her. She wasn't a sexy babe. She was a mother. A widow.

A woman in desperate need of a cut and color.

Years ago she'd been cute, flirty and fun. But hard times had sucked the joy out of her. Amy couldn't even recall the last time she'd laughed until tears had filled her eyes.

Another fifteen minutes passed and she worried that Matt intended to skip lunch, so she decided to make him a sandwich. The phone rang in the middle of slathering mayonnaise on a hoagie bun.

"Amy here."

"You lucky dog, you."

"Chrissy?"

"How come your best friend—" best friend—yeah, right. Chrissy owned the Snappy Scissors Hair Salon in Pebble Creek and believed every woman within a fifty-mile radius was her best friend "—is the last to hear you're involved with that stud—"

"SOS is—"

"Not that stud," Chrissy cut in. "The two-legged one on your farm."

Amy's eyes shifted to the window. "Who's talking about me now?" She wondered if the local gossip-mongers would ever tire of discussing *poor, naive Amy*.

"He didn't tell you?"

"Quit teasing me and spit it out, Chrissy."

"Your rodeo cowboy—" Matt wasn't Amy's cowboy "—broke Payton Scott's nose."

Oh, Lord. "What happened?"

"They exchanged words at the feed store. Clifford says that when he came out of the stockroom Payton was bleeding like a stuck pig and your Matt—"

"He's *not* my Matt."

"—acted madder than a hornet with its stinger plucked. Anyway, Pearl said—"

"What does Pearl have to do with this?" Had the entire town gotten involved?

"Matt stopped at Pearl's after he left the feed store. She claims they were fighting over you."

Amy's heart sighed. Maybe it was silly to feel all wishy-washy inside that Matt had thrown a punch on her behalf, but she'd never been the cause of a dis-agreement between two men. "Do you know what started the fight?"

"Payton maligned your character."

The jerk had probably called her a slut. Payton had a nasty habit of slandering women who didn't appreciate his interest. Maybe Matt's encounter with the banker was the reason he hadn't come up to the house for lunch. "My relationship with Matt Cartwright is purely professional. He's here to save SOS from the slaughterhouse and nothing more."

"What if he wants more?" the beautician hinted.

"A cowboy like Matt doesn't want a woman like me, besides—" The rest of her sentence gurgled in her throat when she spotted Matt watching her through the screen door. How long had he been eavesdropping? "Gotta run." Amy hung up on the sputtering hairdresser.

Matt's eyes pinned Amy.

She concentrated on taking short, quick breaths and keeping her gaze from straying to the wall of sweating muscle a few feet away. He was dusty and so damned *hot*-looking. She managed in a reasonable voice, "I was about to bring you a sandwich."

He stepped into the kitchen.

"You can wash up at the sink." She forgot to hold her breath when she skirted him and caught a whiff of hardworking male and faded aftershave. Resisting the temptation to bury her nose against his sweaty neck, and get drunk on his scent, she snatched a bag of chips from the pantry shelf. "What would you like to drink?"

"Water's fine."

She took a tumbler from the cupboard, filled it with ice and ran the tap.

"Aren't you eating?" he said, taking a seat at the table. His Adam's apple bobbed as he guzzled the water.

"I had a sandwich earlier." With her stomach tied in knots, anything she consumed now she'd regurgitate.

"A man like Matt doesn't want—" his blue eyes narrowed "—what?"

"Chrissy from the hair salon in town likes to run off at the mouth."

"She told you I punched Scott."

"Did you really break his nose?" Amy whispered.

"Yep." He bit off a hunk of sandwich and chewed. *Don't ask.* "Why did you hit him?"

He chewed and swallowed. "I didn't like the things he insinuated about you."

Matt's words were poetry to her ears. "I appreciate you defending me, but Payton has insulted every resident in Pebble Creek at one time or another. No one pays him any mind."

A sexy dark eyebrow lifted at the outer corner. "You don't mind being referred to as a hussy?"

Her face heated. "Is that what Payton called me?"

Matt nodded.

The banker was the biggest poop this side of the Mississippi. Agitated, she grabbed a handful of paper towels and the Windex bottle from beneath the sink, then took out her frustration on the dirty kitchen windows. "Next time ignore the Neanderthal."

"There won't be a next time. If there is…I'll knock his teeth down his throat," Matt pledged.

A tiny fissure spread through Amy's heart. Ben would never have come to her defense the way Matt had. "Payton was three years ahead of me in high school. He came from an affluent family and, well, I came from the farm. So when he showed interest in me I was excited and asked him to the Sadie Hawkins dance." She shook her head. "Big mistake. He acted like he was God's gift to women, bragging about his athletic ability, his academic rank and his family's money. We didn't go out again and I was glad when he left for college."

"Why'd he return to Pebble Creek?" Matt asked.

"His daddy owns several banks in Idaho and built the one in town so his son would have a job. When Payton graduated from college I was already married to Ben. Payton acted as if I'd betrayed him."

"The guy sounds like a nutcase."

"He is."

Matt polished off his sandwich, then took his dishes to the sink. He paused at the screen door. "For the record—" his eyes warmed as they slid over her body "—a man like Matt *does* want."

The banging of the screen door reminded Amy that she'd stopped breathing, and she gasped for air.

Chapter Eight

"Here's the deal," Matt said, handing Rose a box of Silly Nillys. "You and your sister sit on the porch swing and eat your snacks while I install this fence." He intended to enclose a small section of shaded yard alongside the house that he had a view of from the corrals. Once the girls were imprisoned, he'd be able to work with SOS uninterrupted. The towheads crawled onto the swing and Matt relocated the pink plastic playhouse to the soon-to-be secured area, away from Amy's flowerbeds.

"Mama's gonna be mad 'cause you moved Lily's castle," Rose warned.

Mama's not going to say a thing if she wants to keep the nanny happy.

Speaking of Amy, Matt didn't know who had been more shocked when he'd all but blurted that he wanted to have sex with her. He told himself that his slip of the tongue had been because he'd wanted her to know she was an attractive woman—he suspected it had been a while since Amy had received a flattering compliment from the opposite sex.

Better he believe that reasoning than admit she stirred him in a way he'd never experienced before. Matt figured it wouldn't take much effort to seduce Amy and a part of him wanted to. But he shouldn't. Couldn't. Wouldn't. She deserved better than him—a cowboy who'd stooped so low as to use another man's weakness to his advantage.

Shoving aside his thoughts, Matt measured the spacing for the fence posts, then used a mallet to pound them into the ground. Rose called his name, but he ignored the kid. After five minutes he gave in. "What?"

"Did you feed Sophia?"

Blasted rat. The first thing he'd done after his trip into town earlier in the day was to set the trap using part of his Reuben sandwich as bait. "Sophia hasn't shown her—" beady red eyes "—face lately."

"That's 'cause she knows you don't like her."

Ignoring the seven-year-old's glare, he continued setting the posts.

"Uh-oh."

Reining in his temper, he faced the porch and snapped, "Now what's wrong?"

"Lily's tooting."

"Then scoot over so you don't smell it."

The suggestion earned him an eye roll. "If Lily toots it means she's gotta go to the bathroom."

"All right. Will you take her inside and help her?"

Rose released a dramatic sigh. "C'mon, Lily. Let's do poops." Rose slid off the bench seat and her sister followed like a puppet on a string. As soon as the screen door slammed shut, Matt breathed a sigh of relief, then took advantage of the peace and quiet and finished positioning the remainder of the posts. Amazing what a man accomplished when females weren't nagging him. He was in the process of stringing the end of the fencing material to the hooks on the posts when Rose called to him through the screen door.

"Mr. Matt!"

"Yeah?"

"You gotta come quick."

"Why?"

"Lily's marbles spilled all over the bathroom floor."

Why in the world were the girls playing with marbles in the bathroom? "I'll be right in." He leaned the roll of fencing against a post and hustled up the porch steps and into the house.

"Mama's gonna be mad at you, Lily. You're supposed to use the toilet."

Matt stopped outside the half bath in the hallway and stared. Lily stood in front of the toilet, underwear around her ankles. Rose perched one hand on her hip and pointed to the mess. "Lily pooped marbles all over the floor."

Oh, man! "Don't move, Lily. Rose, stay put so you don't step on the…marbles." He scratched his head, wondering how to proceed with the cleanup.

"Mama throws the marbles back in the toilet," Rose commented.

He scooped up Lily, intending to set her in the hall when he noticed several marbles stuck to her underwear. He swung her over the toilet and jiggled her. The kid grinned, then demanded, "Again."

What the heck. He jiggled.

She giggled. "Again."

Jiggle-giggle.

One by one the marbles plopped into the toilet. Matt put Lily on her feet in the hallway. Then he grabbed a wad of toilet paper and shoved it at Rose. "Wipe your sister's bottom."

Rose crossed her arms in front of her. "Yuck."

Matt handed the tissue to Lily. "Clean yourself, Lily."

The kid bent forward at the waist, sticking her fanny high in the air, then tried to wipe herself, but her short little arms didn't reach around to her bottom. "Turn around, Lily."

The child swiveled until her fanny faced Matt. "Never mind, it looks pretty clean." He took the tissue from Lily's hand and used it to retrieve the marbles from the floor. "Rose, pull up Lily's underwear, would you?"

While Rose struggled with her sister's clothing, Matt flushed the toilet. One crisis over. "Hustle outside now."

"Lily's gotta wash her hands."

Where was the antibacterial hand gel when you needed it? He held the child over the sink and helped her soap and rinse her hands. "Shake 'em dry, kid." Lily obeyed, flinging her wet hands every which way.

"Aren't you gonna scrub the floor?" Rose asked.

Good idea. "Where's your mother's cleaning stuff?"

"In the pantry." The little drill sergeant led the way to the kitchen.

Matt searched the meager supplies and settled on the Windex bottle. He sprayed the floor liberally, wiped it with paper towels, then ushered the girls to the swing. Twenty minutes later he had the fence installed.

Next on his list—the bell.

Rose wandered closer and peered inside the box. "What's that?"

"A bell to ring in an emergency."

"What kind of emergency?"

"If you or Lily get hurt playing in the yard, then you ring the bell. I'll hear it and come running."

"But I can come get you," she argued.

"No. You and your sister have to stay inside the fence."

"Why?"

"So I can work with the horses."

Lily joined Rose in the discussion. "Bell." She pointed a sticky finger at the box.

Rose scrutinized the fence as if unhatching an escape plan. She confirmed his suspicion. "All I gotta do is lift up the bottom and crawl under."

"You better not, young lady. I'm depending on you to keep an eye on Lily." A twinge of guilt pricked him. Amy hadn't left him in charge so that he'd shove his responsibilities off on her eldest daughter.

"But I don't want to babysit Lily."

"You're not really babysitting her, you're playing together."

"What if I don't want to play with her?" Rose's mouth formed a pout.

Lily pulled on her sister's shirt sleeve. "Ro, play."

Rose tugged free of Lily's hold. "What about my spelling words?"

"I'll quiz you over supper."

"When's supper?"

God help me. "After I work an hour with the horses,

we'll eat." A couple more screws and Matt had installed the bell on the porch post within the girls' reach.

"Can I ring it first?" Rose asked.

"Give it a try."

Clang! Clang! Clang!

"Me," Lily demanded, pushing Rose out of the way. After several more ear-splitting clangs, he grabbed the clapper. "This isn't a toy, okay? You ring it when you need help. Any questions?"

Rose shook her head. "Nope."

"Nope," Lily mimicked.

Then Matt remembered the walkie-talkies in the truck. "One more thing." He shuffled down the steps, walked three feet, then came to a dead stop. *Oh, hell.* He'd barricaded himself inside the yard.

"Stay here," he insisted, after he climbed the steps. He hurried through the house, reminding himself to install a lock on the screen door to keep the girls from going into the house, then exiting through the front door. The situation was becoming more complicated than plotting a military coup. Once he retrieved the walkie-talkies and installed the batteries, he called the girls over to the fence.

"This is a two-way radio, Rose." He lifted the handset above the fence. "We can talk to each other when I'm in the barn or inside the corral. Press this button on the side and then hold it in place while you speak. When you're done talking release the button."

He walked over to the shade tree outside the fence and hid behind it. "This is Mr. Matt, come in." When Rose didn't answer he peeked around the trunk. "Push the button in and hold it while you talk."

"Hi, Mr. Matt. Can you hear me?"

He leaned around the trunk. "Let go of the button now." When she did, he said, "I can hear you, Rose."

"Lily wants to talk."

A second later... "Mer Matt, Mer Matt."

Rose remembered to release the button and he answered, "Hi, Lily." Then he joined the girls. "Put this strap around your waist, Rose. That way you'll have the walkie-talkie with you at all times." He reached over the fence and helped her tighten the carrying belt. "You girls behave while I work with the horses."

"Bye, Mr. Matt," Rose spoke into the handset, then crawled inside the playhouse, Lily trailing behind.

His focus on the stallion, Matt entered the corral. SOS tensed, but didn't shy away when Matt closed the distance between them. The mares were beginning to show signs of coming into season. If all went well, Matt assumed the mares would be pregnant by the end of June.

Then he'd leave the Broken Wheel and Amy and the girls behind. If he hadn't already blown most of his savings on the mares he'd offer to take SOS off her hands and save Amy the trouble of finding a buyer. He'd have to call in a few favors with his rodeo buddies and see if any of the guys knew a rancher who might be interested in the stud. The sooner the animal was gone from the property the sooner Amy's clients would return to board their horses at the farm.

When Matt drew within ten feet of the stallion, he veered away and stopped next to the saddle he'd draped over the top of the corral earlier in the day. He'd hoped SOS would wander over to investigate the tack. Matt made as much noise as possible, handling the buckles and the cinch. After five minutes SOS wandered closer. Matt held his ground.

"Mr. Matt, can you hear me?" Rose's voice squawked through the walkie-talkie. SOS reared and Matt scrambled to avoid the horse's hooves. Then the stallion bolted to the opposite end of the corral. Matt adjusted the volume lower on the handset. "What's the problem?"

"We're bored."

He rubbed his brow, feeling a banger of a headache coming on. "Why don't you play with your dolls?"

"Wait a minute." Rose forgot to release the button and he heard her ask, "Lily, do you want to play dolls?"

"No," Lily shouted.

"Mr. Matt, can you hear me?"

Once she released the button, he answered. "Yes, I can hear you, Rose."

"Lily doesn't want to play dolls."

"How about coloring?" Amy kept a large coffee can filled with crayons on the kitchen counter.

"How long do we have to color for?" Rose asked.

He'd better cut short his time with the stallion. Once the girls became accustomed to the new setup, he'd be able to work for longer periods of time. "Color for thirty minutes."

"Okay, bye."

He let out a deep breath, then carried the saddle toward SOS. The stallion trotted away. Matt repeated the drill five times—advancing on the stud with saddle in hand—before SOS stood his ground and didn't run.

"Hey, cowboy." A sultry voice reached Matt's ear. "This is magic fingers, over."

Matt noticed a small, compact car parked in front of the house. Caught up in working with the horse he hadn't heard the vehicle approach. Why hadn't Rose rung the bell to warn him they had a visitor?

"How about you come on up to the house for a chitchat? Over."

He searched the porch area and found a redhead sitting on the swing between the girls.

Damn it. He didn't have time for a *chitchat*. "Be right there," he grumbled into the handset. He placed the saddle aside and left the corral. "Can I help you?" he asked, stopping outside the safety fence.

The redhead spoke into the walkie-talkie even though she'd heard him just fine. "I'm Chrissy. Over." Matt frowned and she set the walkie-talkie aside. "I own the Snappy Scissors Hair Salon in town."

The hairdresser wore more makeup than a rodeo clown. "Amy's not here."

"I know. She's at class." The woman winked. "Decided to drop by and offer my help with the girls."

He wasn't about to look a gift horse in the mouth. "Thanks. The girls are hungry. Maybe you can feed them." He'd taken three steps when she protested.

"Oh, I can't stay that long!"

Figured as much.

The woman crossed the porch, her eyes glued to Matt's chest. He was glad he'd kept his shirt on this afternoon. He didn't mind Amy's eyes devouring him, but the redhead's leer made him uncomfortable. "I stopped by to invite you to bring the girls into town for a complimentary haircut."

"Amy should really be the one to—"

"Amy hasn't been to my salon since before Christmas." Chrissy sashayed down the steps. "She doesn't have the money to pay for the girls' haircuts. I'd like to surprise her."

The hairdresser glanced away, convincing Matt that the free-haircut offer had nothing to do with helping Amy and everything to do with getting him into her salon.

"Rose and Lily, you want new hairdos?" Chrissy called over her shoulder.

Lily clapped her hands. "New do! New do!"

Rose ran over to the fence. "Can we, Mr. Matt? Chrissy paints my fingernails when I get a haircut."

"Not right now, Rose. I'm busy." He didn't appreciate the hairdresser using the kids to get her way.

"C'mon, Mr. Matt," the woman purred, batting her eyelashes. "I promise a trim won't take long."

"Please, Mr. Matt. Please," Rose begged.

He was no match for the little girl's pleading eyes and praying hands. "I'll bring the girls by after supper."

Chrissy flashed a smile. "Great. See you then." She waltzed up the porch steps and straight into the house, then exited through the front door and sauntered to her car, her hips swinging.

God help him—couldn't a cowboy train a horse without females interfering?

Drat.

Amy stood next to pump four at the Gas Depot on the outskirts of Pebble Creek, filling her tank when the town busybody spotted her and waved.

"Hello, Amy." Francine Willington bypassed her

black 1975 Oldsmobile Delta convertible and headed in Amy's direction. The woman's steel-gray bob hugged her head like a leather football helmet from the olden days.

Amy's fingers squeezed the trigger tighter, forcing the fuel to flow faster into the gas tank. "Buying lottery tickets?" she asked.

"Have them right here." A blue-veined hand waved the proof in the air. The seventy-year-old widow lived in constant fear of becoming destitute. Not even the three million dollars her husband left her when he'd died a few years ago was enough to ease Francine's fears, so she spent a hundred dollars a month on Quick Picks. *Kooky old woman.*

"I must say, Amy, I never expected you to move on so soon after Ben died."

Excuse me?

Francine lowered her voice and leaned forward. "I don't blame you though. If a man as handsome as that cowboy had come along before Harold had died—" the widow snapped her fingers "—I would have snatched him right up." She winked. "Rich men can be a bit boring, you know."

Oh, brother. "Where did you meet Matt?"

"I stopped in at the Snappy Scissors to make a hair appointment a few minutes ago and your cowboy and the girls were getting haircuts."

Chrissy…*darn her.* Jealousy zapped Amy and she glanced at her hand, surprised her fingers hadn't let off sparks. Why was she shocked Matt had fallen under Chrissy's spell? *Because this morning he'd said…*"a man like Matt does want." *Fickle cowboy.*

Most rodeo cowboys had their pick of gorgeous women. The day she'd met Ben, a dozen flirty females had been buzzing around him. Matt was twice as handsome and ten times more successful than her husband had been. Still…Matt had given Amy the impression he was interested in *her*.

The pump clicked off and she stowed the handle. "I've gotta run, Francine. Have a good day." She skirted the old woman, glancing inside the convertible as she walked past. Sitting in the drink holder was Francine's favorite beer—a bottle of Budweiser. Someone really ought to take the woman's car keys away. Amy paid for the gas inside the store, then returned to her truck, intent on dropping by the beauty salon. Someone—her—needed to make sure Chrissy understood her daughters' babysitter was off-limits.

Less than two minutes later, the bell above the door announced her arrival when she stepped into the Snappy Scissors.

"Mama!" Lily squealed from her booster seat in a styling chair, where Sara, a part-time stylist, brushed the tangles from her curls.

"Hi, sweetie."

"We're getting haircuts. Even Mr. Matt." Rose pointed to the chair next to her. Annie, the other part-time stylist was trimming Rose's bangs.

Gathering her courage Amy looked at Matt. Chrissy's fingers were buried deep in his hair, giving him one of her famous scalp massages for an extra two dollars—only he was likely getting it for free.

"You're home early. Anything wrong?" Matt closed his eyes and groaned.

Traitor.

Chrissy spun the chair, presenting Amy with Matt's back. Then the stylist had the audacity to lean forward and smash her Double-D boobs against his shoulder.

"Nothing's wrong," Amy said. "The professor had an emergency and class was cut short." She pulled in a deep breath through her nose, but the extra oxygen did little to calm her frustration. "I skipped a study session with my classmates in order to give you more time to work with SOS. Had I known you'd decided to play beauty parlor this afternoon, I'd have stayed in Rockton."

Matt shifted toward Amy, but Chrissy flattened her palm against his cheek, keeping his face forward. "Quit wiggling."

Sara and Annie pretended to fuss with the girls' hair, but Amy wasn't fooled. The two women eavesdropped on every word. They probably hadn't seen their boss tussle over a man in ages.

The fact that Amy even considered *tussling* over Matt convinced her that she'd lost her mind. Cowboys were nothing but trouble.

"Amy." Chrissy motioned to the magazine rack in the waiting area. "Check out the article on makeovers in the *Glamour* magazine."

Ha. Ha. The former rodeo queen's insult didn't bother her in the least. Amy was well aware of her unremarkable appearance. What hurt was having her faults pointed out in front of Matt. That she wanted him to find her attractive and desirable convinced her she was headed for heartbreak. *Stupid. Stupid. Stupid.*

Hadn't she already decided she'd never depend on a

man again? The closer she became to Matt the more she'd be tempted to lean on him—then where would she be when he cut out on her? No ifs, ands or buts about it—becoming involved with the cowboy would eventually leave her with scars deeper than Hells Canyon.

Amy took a seat in the waiting area and glowered at Chrissy, who continued to massage Matt's head. If the beautician rubbed much harder his scalp would peel off. When Sara and Annie finished with the girls they handed out lollipops. Amy approached the register, swallowing a groan at having to use the last of her gas money to pay for haircuts.

"Put your wallet away," Chrissy demanded. "The cuts are complimentary." She winked. "You three mosey along. Matt's going to be here a while longer."

"Let's go, girls." She ushered them to the door, worried if she didn't leave she'd grab a pair of scissors and gouge Chrissy's eyes out.

"Wait, Amy." Matt tossed his truck keys across the room and she caught them in midair. "The car seat," he reminded her.

Without another word, she and the girls departed. As they walked around the side of the building to the parking lot, Amy's attempt to talk herself into feeling bad about not thanking Chrissy for the girls' cuts bombed. The hairdresser's graciousness had been stained by ulterior motive. Chrissy wanted Matt and wasn't above using Rose and Lily to achieve her goal.

Until this moment Amy had never believed herself the jealous type. Not even the few times she'd accompanied Ben to a rodeo and had witnessed the scantily clad groupies flirting with him had she been this envious. The sudden attack of the green monster worried her. "Nuts."

"What's nuts?" Rose asked.

"Nothing, honey." *Hormones.* Blaming her chaotic feelings on a sudden spike in her estrogen level was safer than contemplating the possibility that she was falling in love with the cowboy camping out in her barn. Her attraction to Matt was purely physical, not emotional.

Yeah, right.

"Mama." Rose tugged Amy's hand.

Amy hadn't realized she'd stopped walking. "Where did Mr. Matt park?" She shielded her eyes against the bright sun and scanned the vehicles in the lot.

Rose pointed to the far corner.

When they reached the truck, Amy balked. Pride demanded she go home to show Matt she could give a flip what he did with the hairdresser. Jealousy, fueled by estrogen, insisted she remain and remind the cowboy that *she* had first dibs on him.

Before she came to a decision, Matt materialized. He glanced at the key fob in her hand. Rose shrugged her slim shoulders as if to say she had no idea why her mother had been staring into space.

Matt covered Amy's hand with his and bleeped the truck locks open. "Do you want me to take the girls or transfer the car seat to your truck?"

Her skin prickled at the sound of his voice. Lord, she had it bad. "You didn't get your haircut."

"Didn't want one."

Did that mean he worried about her feelings? "I guess the girls can ride with you," she said.

"Big girls first." He lifted Rose into the truck, then deposited Lily in the car seat.

While he buckled the girls in, it occurred to Amy how at ease her daughters had become with Matt. She hadn't given much thought to how the girls would react when Matt loaded his mares into the horse trailer and drove out of their lives forever. Time to devise a new nanny game plan. She might not be able to protect her heart from Matt, but she had to do everything in her power to save the girls from suffering a similar heartache.

"Shit, Ro."

Amy gasped.

Matt slammed the truck door, a stunned expression on his face.

"Did you hear that?" she asked.

"Hear what?"

"Lily said a swear word."

"You must have misheard," Matt insisted.

"I didn't mishear anything. Lily said *S-H-I-T*." Amy squinted. "I wonder who she heard that from?"

"Forget the swear word." Matt paused in front of her. "Are we going to talk about it? Or are you going to pretend it doesn't exist?"

"Talk about what?" She tilted her head to make eye contact.

"This." He leaned in and brushed his lips across hers, then pulled away—too soon.

Her heart stumbled, then regained its balance as she quickly scanned the area, fearing one of the locals had witnessed the kiss. Thank goodness they were alone in the parking lot.

"We're attracted to each other," he stated.

She shook her head.

"Deny it all you want, Amy. But it's there in your eyes."

Oh, she was in deep horse hockey.

"I know you watch me through the kitchen window." He moved closer, edging her away from the truck windows where the girls could see. "Why do you think I've been working with my shirt off?"

Oh, God.

He flashed a cocky half grin and she locked her knees in hopes of preventing an embarrassing swoon.

"But…but…Chrissy," she blubbered like an idiot.

"What about her?"

"She wants you, too." Great. Now he knew Amy was jealous of the beautician.

Blue eyes smoldering, he whispered, "I don't want Chrissy."

Amy felt the swoon approaching and clasped his arms for balance. She lifted her face, gulping air as she waited for his mouth…his lips…

"For better or worse…I want *you*." He kissed her again, this time his tongue sweeping the inside of her mouth before pulling away. Then he hopped into the truck, revved the engine and left Amy standing in the parking lot with her lips aching for more.

Chapter Nine

Amy awoke Saturday morning around five, swung her feet to the floor, sat up and rubbed her eyes. After years of rising early to tend to horses, she'd yet to reset her body's internal clock. The past few months she'd replaced barn chores with sipping coffee on the porch swing, watching the sunrise and worrying over bills.

She stretched her arms high above her head, then shoved herself off the mattress and padded across the hall to the bathroom. Matt's aftershave and deodorant lingered in the air, their scents strangely comforting—as if he'd been showering and shaving in her bathroom years instead of mere days. In less than five minutes she had her face washed, moisturized and her teeth brushed. The sound of a horse whinny drew her to the window.

Against a canvas of pink sky and misty air, Matt rode SOS around the corral. The cowboy had been true to his word—although it had taken two weeks instead of one—he'd succeeded in riding the stallion.

Which meant…Matt was staying. At least a month. Maybe longer.

And he wants you.

Excitement quickened her pulse. Amy had a decision to make—to sleep or not to sleep with Matt. She closed her eyes and conjured up an image of his naked body. Where men were concerned, Amy hadn't even driven halfway around the block. Shoot, she'd barely left the driveway and her lack of relationship experience didn't bode well for her heart.

Blame her blunder with Ben on infatuation. She'd fallen in love with the aura that surrounded rodeo cowboys—their toughness, their swaggers, their killer smiles. And Matt carried off the image far better than Ben had. She was too young to label Matt a midlife crisis. The word *fling* sounded crass. A summer affair…maybe.

Was she setting herself up for heartbreak? *Most definitely.* But Matt had been the first man in forever to make her believe everything would be fine—she'd land a good job, reopen her boarding business, pay off her debt and keep the farm.

The stallion trotted in circles and Matt patted the stud's neck in encouragement. How long would he wait for her to give him a signal that she was ready to make love? No matter that he claimed he wasn't interested in the local hairdresser, Amy feared if she didn't make a move soon, Chrissy would change Matt's mind.

First things first—clothes and coffee. She shimmied into a pair of jeans and a T-shirt, then slid her bare feet into sandals. The smell of coffee teased her nose when she reached the first-floor landing. She could become accustomed to having a man around who knew how to brew a decent cup of coffee.

She sipped her first cup standing at the kitchen sink, enjoying the view of her flower garden. The mass of bluebells had begun to fade and nearby pink tulip petals littered the ground. But her sprawling knapweed with their furry leaves and blue and purple flowers thrived among the white columbine. She'd wanted to expand the garden to include a walking path and a sitting area, but debt had put those plans on hold.

A swell of sadness brought tears to her eyes. Even though she and Ben had had their share of troubles, she'd never wished for his life to have ended in such a tragic way. Now she'd never know if Ben might have kicked his gambling habit—not that it would have changed their future. Amy had fallen out of love with Ben pretty darn quick after Rose had been born. After Lily's birth, Amy had hoped Ben would change his ways. He hadn't, so she'd contacted a lawyer to begin divorce proceedings. Ben had died before the lawyer had finished drawing up the paperwork.

What's done is done.

After pouring a second cup of coffee, she headed for the porch, then stopped and reversed direction, walking through the house and out the front door. When they'd returned to the farm after haircuts and she spotted the orange safety fence strung around the yard, she hadn't known what to think. Matt had stumbled through an explanation, aided by Rose: "It's a fence so Lily and I won't get in the way." Amy failed to see the logic in Matt's plan—if the girls wanted to escape all they had to do was walk out the front door.

Then Lily had pointed out the bell attached to the porch post and had clanged the thing until everyone's ear drums begged for relief. Matt had insisted the bell was to be used for emergencies and it had taken ev-

erything inside Amy not to point out that there would
be no emergencies if he stayed with the girls and made
sure neither of them got hurt.

Later while Matt was in the barn and she and the
girls sat on the swing, Rose had pulled out a walkie-
talkie and said, "Horse Tamer, this is Wild Rose, over."

Matt had responded with, "I hear you loud and
clear, Wild Rose. You and Lily Pad okay? Over."

Horse Tamer, Wild Rose and Lily Pad. *Good grief.*
Amy had grabbed the walkie-talkie from her daughter
and had chimed in with, "Horse Tamer this is Betty
Crocker. Vittles'll be ready soon. Over."

For the next ten minutes they'd all goofed off with
the walkie-talkies, Matt amazing her with his patience
when they'd interrupted him in the middle of chores.
Amy admired many things about Matt, but it was his
gentle demeanor with Rose and Lily that elevated him
to hero status in her eyes. And she feared in their eyes,
too.

As soon as Amy rounded the side of the house,
Matt spotted her and waved. She moseyed up to the
corral and quietly observed cowboy and horse. The
animal's dark coat gleamed in the sun and his refined
head, long neck and muscular hindquarters were evi-
dence of his thoroughbred genes as was the rebellious
streak he exhibited when he refused to dance sideways
at Matt's command.

Sitting loose in the saddle, Matt's hips rocked with
the stallion's rhythmic gait. He put SOS through several stop-and-go maneuvers and the animal responded
beautifully. Then rider and horse rode over to her and
she held her breath, wondering…hoping…he'd kiss

her. The air whooshed from her lungs when he leaned forward and…grabbed the coffee cup from her hand.

"Thanks," he said. Then after a sip, he declared, "That hit the spot."

Disappointed, she nodded at the horse. "I guess congratulations are in order."

The grin he flashed rivaled the sunrise. "I never had a doubt that I'd be able to ride him."

She offered her hand for a sniff and SOS nuzzled her fingers. "He hardly seems like the same stallion."

"Cinnamon—" Matt pointed to the chestnut mare "—is coming into season. I'm going to release her into the pasture, then later this morning I'll let SOS out and see what he does. If he behaves like a gentleman I'll set him free and let the two get on with business. If he doesn't, then I'll bring him back to the corral."

After a strained silence, he asked, "What are your plans today?"

"Housecleaning, laundry, homework." *And watching you.*

"Exciting."

"Story of my life." She brushed a strand of hair from her cheek. "Since we're sharing good news…I found a babysitter. Jake's wife, Helen, phoned this past Thursday and said her neighbor's granddaughter was visiting for the summer and hoping to earn a little spending money. Nicole's a sophomore in college."

"Have you met the girl?"

"I stopped by the Gundersons' last night on the way home from class. Nicole should be able to handle the girls, but if you notice—"

"Don't worry. I'll keep an eye on the three of them."

He motioned to the gaudy orange safety fence. "Want me to get rid of that?"

"Let's leave it up a day or two." Not because it served any real purpose, but because it reminded Amy of Matt and his goofy babysitting tactics. Her eyes drifted to his mouth. "What are your plans after you work with SOS?"

"I don't have any. Why?"

She scuffed the toe of her sandal in the dirt. "Thought I'd take the girls on a picnic. Care to join us?"

"Can't think of a better way to spend my lunch hour than with three lovely ladies."

Heat rushed into Amy's face. "We're leaving at eleven-thirty."

"I'll be ready." As he rode off, Amy decided his backside was as impressive as the front side.

MATT RECLINED NEXT TO AMY on the blanket they'd spread beneath the scraggly arms of a sprawling kwanza cherry tree. Ten yards away the girls splashed in a trickling creek. "This is what Oklahoma is missing," Matt said, staring at Amy's profile.

"What's that?"

You. "Green. Lots of rich, green vegetation."

She rolled her head to the side and her lashes fluttered up. "I don't think I'd like living in Oklahoma."

"Ever been to the Sooner State?"

She shook her head. "The weather's a little wild for my taste. I'll take a raging blizzard over a tornado any day."

Matt studied his surroundings—a verdant valley dotted with white pine, ponderosa and Douglas fir—

and decided this wasn't such a bad place to raise horses. He shifted his attention to Amy. She was as rich and curvy as the Idaho terrain. How had he ever believed this woman plain-looking?

"You should have let me pack a lunch instead of spending money on takeout from the café in town," she murmured, staring at the canopy of branches overhead.

Matt didn't dare confess he'd called Pearl each day this past week to place a take-out order for him and the girls. He'd even tipped Pearl handsomely to drop the food off at the bus stop near the end of Amy's driveway. The girls hadn't asked why he drove to the road each day after their mother had left for class—they'd been easily distracted with Silly Nillys.

He turned on his side, bumping Amy's hip with his thigh, then he leaned over her and angled his head for a kiss.

"The girls." Her words sighed across his lips.

A quick glance sideways confirmed that the little munchkins were busy picking dandelions. "They're fine." Amy's eyes closed and Matt took that as a *yes,* pressing his mouth to hers. Nothing heavy. A brushing of lips—enough to warm his blood, raise his testosterone level and jump-start his pulse. When the cool, wet glide of Amy's tongue slid across his lower lip, he moved his hand to the front of her blouse and thumbed her nipple.

Then Lily squealed and Amy jerked upright, almost knocking him in the mouth with the top of her head. "Sorry." Her breathless apology did nothing to ease the ache in his groin. Eyes focused on the girls, she said, "Tell me about your family."

The question about family dissolved the erogenous haze hanging over Matt as bad memories accompanied the sudden cooling of his body. *Amy's not Kayla.* Deep inside Matt believed Amy wasn't a user. Nor was she a liar. And she sure as heck wasn't deceitful. Amy was as clear as the blue sky above their heads. Regardless…being burned tended to make a man cynical and wary.

From the get-go, Kayla had peppered Matt with questions about his father and siblings. He'd stupidly believed her curiosity with his family had been genuine because she'd been adopted—later, after he'd lost his heart to her, he discovered she'd lied about that and whole lot of other things.

"I have a sister—Samantha—she's a couple years younger than me. She works in my father's office, but I have a feeling it won't be long before she quits."

"Why's that?"

"My father sticks his nose into our business way too often. Becomes annoying after a while."

"Is that why you're here?" She brushed a crumb off the blanket. "Because your father got on your nerves?"

The urge to confide in Amy got the best of him. "I want to retire from rodeo and raise cutting horses, but my father would rather I work in the oil business with him." Amy remained silent, so he continued. "I've made a fair amount of money rodeoing over the years, but contrary to popular belief, I don't receive an allowance from my father."

"I get it. He's rich—you're not."

"I have a trust fund, but my father refuses to release the money because he doesn't approve of horses, cattle or much else aside from crude oil." Matt hesitated before deciding to confess everything. "I used most of my savings to buy those mares. If they don't become pregnant—"

"They will." She squeezed his hand. He wished he felt as positive. "So it's just you and your sister?" she asked.

"Nope. I have a stepbrother, Duke, who's one year older. My mother took off when Sam and I were young, and I was already fifteen when Dad married Duke's mom. Duke recently moved his IT company to Detroit, and this past February he married Renée, a social worker. They're in the process of building a shelter for homeless kids that my father's helping to fund."

"Sounds as if your father is a generous man."

The comment rang sincere, but Matt's suspicion radar bleeped, warning him that Amy might be hinting at a Cartwright donation to help get her out of debt.

"If the mares don't conceive, will you continue rodeoing?"

"Before I competed this past December at the NFR, I had serious reservations about continuing my career."

"Why?"

"A combination of things." He rubbed his shoulder— the one he'd landed on a few too many times over the years when he'd taken a fall from his horse. "Mostly I'm getting old. The bumps and bruises don't heal as quickly." And if he was honest with himself he'd admit that Kayla's deception had sucked the joy out of the sport for Matt. Maybe with time, the memory of her lies would fade. "You ever long for a do-over in life?" he asked.

"If I hadn't gone off with Ben to that hotel room all those years ago I wouldn't have Rose or Lily." She offered a soft smile. "Ben wasn't such a bad guy. He was kind to the girls when he was around. And for a while he was succeeding in kicking his gambling habit. The Gamblers Anonymous meetings helped, but—" she sighed "—then he went to Pocatello and fell off the wagon."

Like a blow to the head, the pain was swift and debilitating. Matt tore his gaze from Amy's forlorn expression. He never wanted her to find out that he'd known about Ben's gambling addiction and had suckered the cowboy into the card game. That *he* was responsible for Ben falling off the wagon.

Initially, Ben had declined to join the poker game—and now Matt knew why. What would Amy think of him if she learned her husband had tried to walk away, but Matt wouldn't let him, cajoling and sweet-talking the man until he caved in and agreed to play? From that moment on, Matt's objective had been to beat Ben so badly that the man would be forced to offer SOS's stud service to clear his debt.

If he had known that Ben was already in debt up to his ears, Matt would have kicked the man out of the poker game—at least that's what he told himself. But the truth was Matt had been so pissed at his father that he'd had one objective that night—his own.

"Mr. Matt, come quick!" Rose called. "I see a fish."

Seizing an excuse to run from the guilty feelings putting a damper on the picnic, Matt sprang from the blanket and joined the girls.

NOW WHAT? AMY STOPPED scrubbing the barbecue grill when she spotted Payton Scott's car barreling up the gravel road, creating a dust cloud that would take a half hour to dissipate. She wasn't in the mood to deal with the egotistical banker.

Ever since she and the girls ended their picnic with Matt earlier in the day, she'd gone about household chores in a stupor, trying to figure out what she'd said or done that had pushed Matt away. They'd been sitting on the blanket talking about his rodeo career and all of a sudden, he'd bolted to the stream. If she didn't know better, Amy would think Matt was hiding something from her.

Payton got out of his car and headed in her direction, his short, zigzagging strides reminding her of a chicken being chased by a dog. He didn't bother to say hello to Rose or Lily, who were drawing with chalk on the stepping stones in her garden. "Amy, we have to talk," he said.

She hid a smile when she noticed the new bump he sported in the middle of his nose and the purple bruises beneath both eyes. Matt sure had messed up the banker's face. "Hello, Payton."

"You've been avoiding me." The smell of his heavy cologne nauseated her. She preferred Matt's crisp, clean aftershave.

"I've been busy." She scrubbed harder at the grime-encrusted grill and refused to feel bad that she hadn't returned his phone calls.

"I may have found a buyer for your farm."

The brush skidded to a stop. "As I said before, I'm not interested in selling."

He flashed a smarmy grin. "You and I both know it's a matter of time before your *cowboy* packs his saddlebags and moves on. Then who will you get to pay your mortgage?"

Amy didn't want to contemplate the day when Matt's mares turned up pregnant and he no longer had a reason to stay. "Who's interested in my farm?"

Payton's gaze slid sideways. "No one you know."

Sounded like the banker was up to no good.

"Your father tried to talk your mother into getting rid of the place," he said.

Amy wasn't surprised. Selling the farm had probably been another one of her father's million-dollar ideas. "Stop pestering me. As long as I make the mortgage payment, the bank can't touch my farm."

"And how long do you think you'll be able to keep up the payments once Cartwright leaves?" He didn't allow her a chance to argue before he asked, "Where's the cowboy?"

"Matt's in the barn grooming SOS."

"You'll never find a buyer for that horse. Word's gotten around that he killed Ben."

And she was certain Payton was responsible for spreading the rumors. "It was an accident."

"Cartwright's got a death wish is what I think." Payton smirked. "When he rides off and leaves you in the dust, give me a call. Though I can't guarantee you'll get as good an offer on the property."

Payton's car hadn't even vanished from sight, when a horse's scream rent the air. "Stay put, girls!" She dropped the grill brush and sprinted toward the barn.

Please let Matt be okay. Please let him be okay.

The horse screams continued and the sound of hooves splintering wood greeted her ears when she entered the barn. Her eyes went straight to SOS's stall. The stud had kicked the door off and was pawing the air. "Matt!" she called, afraid to move closer. *Oh, God.* Where was he? Her stomach churned with dread.

A second later the stallion's hoof broke the latch on the door at the back of the stall and it swung open. SOS bolted into the corral. Heart racing, Amy rushed forward.

"Matt." She found him slumped in the corner, clutching his thigh.

Eyes glazed with pain, he whispered, "I know what sets off SOS."

"What?" She halfheartedly listened as she squatted by his side and ran her fingers through his hair, searching for bumps or lacerations. When she moved her hands to his leg, he swatted them away.

"Rats," he grunted as Amy helped him to his feet. Winded and in obvious pain, he bent at the waist and gulped air. "The rat must have snuck into the stall when Ben was in with SOS."

"What rat? I haven't seen a barn rat around here in ages," she argued.

"Rose's pet rat."

Assuming he'd whacked his head against the stall, Amy spoke slowly. "Rose doesn't have a pet rat."

Matt nodded toward the far corner of the stall and Amy's breath froze in her lungs when she spotted the squashed remains of a large black rodent.

"She didn't want to tell you, but she's been feeding Sophia for a while."

Sophia? Her daughter had named the varmint as if it were her...*pet.*

Dear God. Amy's chest tightened with guilt. Her daughter had befriended a rat because Amy hadn't allowed her to have a dog. If Rose ever found out Sophia had played a role in Ben's death she'd be devastated.

Chapter Ten

Damn. Damn. Damn. Matt's leg ached like a hell.

Using Amy as a walking stick, he limped out of the barn. The fact that he was able to put any weight on his leg reassured him the stallion hadn't shattered the bone.

As he trudged along the gravel drive toward the house, his mind replayed the incident over and over. Matt had entered the stall and shut the door. SOS had stood calmly while Matt brushed his coat—a routine he'd begun a week ago and one that the horse enjoyed.

When Matt had moved to the horse's rump, that's when things had become dicey. SOS whinnied, then shifted restlessly. Matt guessed the horse had caught the rat's scent before the rodent had slipped into the stall. In less than a few seconds, SOS had gone from nervous to crazed.

Thank God Matt had been standing to the horse's side when the stud jumped and kicked out. The hoof had glanced off Matt's thigh, but the force of the impact sent him crashing into the side of the pen, knocking the breath from him. He'd managed to roll out of the way and avoid a stomping until the stallion had kicked the lock off the stall door and broke free.

"I'm calling a doctor." Amy's pronouncement barely registered through the haze of pain fogging his brain.

"What happened, Mr. Matt?" Rose asked when they paused at the bottom of the porch steps. Showing no interest in the adults, Lily continued to draw with chalk.

"Bruised my leg is all," he answered.

"Oh." Apparently satisfied with his explanation, Rose rejoined her sister in the garden.

"Ready?" Amy's breath puffed heavily against his neck.

Six steps—six humungous steps. He clutched the handrail. "Let's do it." His injured leg almost buckled and he choked on a cuss word. By the time he reached the landing his muscles shook with fatigue.

"Sit," Amy ordered as soon as they entered the kitchen. He didn't have the energy to argue. "Take these." She set a glass of water on the table and a bottle of Naproxen. He took four of the anti-inflammatory pills.

"Let's get your jeans off before your leg swells and I have to cut you out of them."

"Interesting pick-up line."

Ignoring his attempt at levity, she said, "The femur may not be broken, but you might have a hairline fracture." She dialed the doctor's number. Matt didn't protest. He was in too much agony to play the tough guy.

After a quick conversation Amy hung up. "Doc Murphy will be here in an hour. He wants you to ice your leg." Amy stood in front of his chair. "Can you manage another set of stairs? You'll be more comfortable lying on a bed than the short couch in the living room."

"If I'd known all I had to do was injure myself to earn an invitation into your bed I'd—"

"Not funny, Matt." Her voice broke, surprising him. "You almost got killed, just like Ben."

What an ass he was not to realize that his injury would remind Amy of her husband's death and trigger memories of that day. He brushed a tear from her cheek. "I'm sorry. I didn't mean—"

"Never mind." She tugged him to his feet.

The trip upstairs left him with a burning sensation in his leg. Amy led him to the room across the hall from the bath. He grabbed the door frame when he spotted a pink bra on the chair in the corner. "This is your bedroom."

"You're too big for Lily's starter bed or Rose's single mattress."

"No guest room?" He glanced at the closed door at the end of the hall.

"The third bedroom is used for storage."

As they crossed the room to Amy's bed, she noticed him eye the pink bra and mumbled, "Sorry." She stuffed the scrap of lace into the top drawer of the bureau, then dropped to her knees in front of him. Before he had the chance to indulge in an erotic fantasy she grabbed his boot heel and jerked. He grunted in pain.

"Sorry." One boot slipped free. Then a second one. He unbuckled his belt and lowered his zipper.

"Aren't you going to close your eyes?" he teased.

The color of her face matched the hot-pink bra she'd hidden from sight. "Can you manage by yourself?"

And miss the chance of her touching him? "Nope." He shoved his jeans past his hips and sat.

"That's going to be a nasty bruise." When her fingers stroked the purplish-red marks marring his thigh, he moaned—the sound having nothing to do with pain and everything to do with her gentle caress. Once she removed his jeans, he reclined on the mattress, and Amy confiscated a blanket from her closet to cover him with.

"I'll fetch the ice." She practically ran from the room.

Less than five minutes later she appeared with a plastic tablecloth, several towels and a pail filled with ice. He frowned at the array of items. "What's all this for?"

"To keep the mattress from getting wet." She snapped open the tablecloth. "Lift up."

He did as ordered, holding his rump in the air until Amy spread the cloth beneath him. Next, she packed ice-filled towels around his thigh, carefully avoiding his crotch, then covered him.

"Thanks." He squeezed her hand and her fingers tightened around his. "I'm going to be fine. Don't worry."

Lips trembling, she begged, "Please don't mention the rat to Rose."

"Of course I won't." Rose would blame herself for her father's death. No child deserved to be burdened with that kind of truth. "It's not her fault, Amy. She didn't know SOS was terrified of rats."

"What's wrong with Mr. Matt?" Rose and Lily strolled into the bedroom. Lily didn't wait for an answer to her sister's question. She charged the bed, bouncing against Matt's injured leg.

Teeth clenched, he swallowed a groan. Amy

scooped Lily up and set her on the floor. "Don't bump him, honey. Mr. Matt injured his leg."

"Does it hurt bad?" Rose asked.

"I'll be good as new in no time." He hated the thought of breaking the news to Rose that Sophia had been trampled to death.

Lily patted his hand. "Boo-boo."

Matt grinned. "Yeah, I've got a big ol' boo-boo, Lily."

"C'mon, girls. Play in your room for a while. Mr. Matt's tired."

Amy ushered her daughters toward the door.

Rose applied the brakes. "I'm hungry."

"I'll make supper soon." After they scampered off, Amy asked, "Anything else I can get for you?"

How about a kiss? Or two. Or three. "No."

"As soon as the doctor arrives, I'll bring him up. If you need me, holler."

He needed Amy all right, but not in the way she meant. Matt must have dozed off because the next time he opened his eyes he saw a short, pudgy man with snow-white hair and Coke-bottle glasses that made his eyes look like giant super balls.

"This is Doc Murphy." Amy stood at the foot of the bed, wringing her hands. "Doc, this is Matt Cartwright." She switched her gaze to Matt. "I told Doc what happened."

The old man whipped out his stethoscope. "That stallion got the best of you, did he?"

"It wasn't the horse's fault," Matt muttered. He didn't want the news of his injury to add to the rumors already going around about SOS.

"Let's have a listen to your lungs. Can you sit up?"

Amy rushed to his side and helped him. Ignoring the gray eyebrow that arched, Matt took deep breaths as instructed.

"Lungs are fine. Let's see the leg."

"I better check on the girls." Amy ducked out of the room.

The doc peeled off the blanket and whistled. "Must hurt like the dickens." He poked and prodded, then rotated Matt's hip socket. "Nothing's broke, except for a heck of a lot of blood vessels." He shook his head. "You're a lucky man, Mr. Cartwright." He pulled out a wicked long needle from his black bag.

"What's that for?"

"This pain medicine will knock you out for a few hours."

"No shots," Matt protested.

"Roll over." Two seconds later, Matt's underwear was yanked down and he winced at the sharp stick in his butt.

"When you wake up walk around a bit to keep the circulation going in your legs. If you have any problems or the pain worsens, have Amy drive you to the E.R. in Rockton. Otherwise, I'll drop by in a few days."

"Thanks, Doc," Matt mumbled, drifting off to sleep.

MATT AWOKE TO AN EERIE silence in the house. The slant of the light through the window proved supper time had passed him by. His bladder complained so he sat up, amazed his injured leg didn't scream in agony—must have been a hell of a shot Doc Murphy had given him. He moved the ice-filled towels aside and swung his legs off the bed.

When the room stopped spinning, he stood and tested his injured limb. Satisfied his leg would support his weight, he hobbled across the floor. A shiver racked his body and he grabbed the door frame to steady himself. After hours packed in ice, his thigh glowed fire-engine red.

He poked his head into the hallway. Coast clear, he hobbled to the bathroom. After finishing his business he considered another nap, but the claw-foot tub beckoned him. First, he'd soak his stiff muscles and warm up in a hot bath, then he'd ask Amy to bring him a snack before his stomach gnawed a hole through his backbone. He grabbed the Mr. Bubble from the toilet tank, stripped, then stepped into the tub and ran the water. He shoved a rolled up towel behind his head and reclined in the hot suds. When the bubbles reached his chin, he shut off the tap and closed his eyes.

"Mer Matt!"

Matt jerked upright, the sudden movement sending a wave of water over the side of the tub, dousing Lily's sandals.

"Uh-oh." Holding a yellow rubber duckie, the little girl lifted her wet foot off the floor.

"Sorry, Lil." Matt snatched another towel from the shelf next to the tub. "Would you wipe up the puddles?"

She shoved the toy at him. "Duck."

"I see that." He exchanged the towel for the duck, then squeaked it. "Thanks for the tub toy."

Bent at the waist, rear in the air, Lily pushed the towel around the wet floor with both hands, spreading water everywhere. "That's good. Thanks, Lil."

Leaving the towel on the floor, she crawled onto the toilet lid and sat.

"Make yourself at home, kid." He grinned and Lily mimicked the gesture.

Amy heard Matt's voice coming from the bathroom when she reached the top of the stairs. She'd been outside in the garden with the girls when she spotted Lily toddling up the porch steps and into the house. After instructing Rose to stay put, Amy had followed her daughter, worried she'd disturb Matt, who'd been sleeping since the doctor had left three hours ago.

Obviously Matt was awake and, from the sound of splashing water, taking a bath. Amy hovered out of sight in the hallway. Spying on the cowboy was becoming a habit—one she didn't mind in the least. She glanced around the door frame and discovered Matt buried beneath a mound of white foam. Plastering herself against the wall in the hallway, she clamped a hand over her mouth to mute her laughter.

"Bubba," Lily said. "Bubba."

"Don't touch the bottle, Lil. We don't want bubble bath spilling all over the floor," Matt warned.

"Me bubba!"

Amy was dying to see who'd win this battle—the cowboy or the two-year-old.

"You'll get your turn later." Matt ran the water in the tub for a few seconds. "Gettin' low on bubbles, Lil. Gotta keep covered."

"Duck."

On cue, Matt squeaked the toy and her daughter laughed. "Hey, I've been meaning to talk to you about that naughty word you said the other day. You got me in a heap o' trouble with your mother."

"Shit, no, no."

Amy swallowed a gasp.

"Don't say that word, okay?"

"'Kay."

"Speaking of your mother…what am I gonna do about her, little Lil?"

The air in Amy's lungs froze.

"I like her. In fact, I like your mom a whole lot. Something about Amy grabs me and doesn't let go. Like you, she's cute and sassy."

"Duck."

Matt squeaked and Lily squealed, "Again!"

Squeak! More giggles.

"I've got this strong urge to protect your mama and help her out of the mess your daddy left her in, but…"

Eager to hear Matt's confession, Amy inched closer to the door.

"I want your mama like nobody's business."

Amy exhaled slowly.

"But if we go all the way, she'll take for granted I'm in it with her forever. And I can't do forever with your mama."

So much for dreaming Matt cared deeply for her.

"You see, Lil, I'm afraid of taking the same road with your mama that I traveled with another woman."

Jealousy surged through Amy.

"Kayla and your mama have a lot in common. At first, Kayla refused my money when her beauty shop hit hard times. But it wasn't long before she changed her mind about accepting a handout from me. Pretty soon she was digging deep into my pockets, but I didn't complain, because I thought we were going to marry." Matt paused. "Guess what, Lil?"

A quick peek inside the bathroom confirmed that her daughter was more interested in the buttons on the front of her shirt than Matt's confession.

"She cheated on me."

"Shit, no, no."

"Lil…that's a naughty word." Matt scowled.

"Shit, naughty," Lily repeated.

"You're right about one thing, Kayla was naughty."

Nausea and anger gripped Amy's stomach. She hurt for Matt, yet at the same time he ticked her off. How dare he believe she was after his money.

Maybe because you asked him to make your mortgage payment?

But she intended to pay back every cent with interest.

"I found Kayla messing around with another cowboy after a rodeo. I didn't know until later that the two had had a kid together, but had never married. And you know the worse part, Lil…?"

"Naughty."

"…was finding out Kayla and her ex had been plotting against me all along. She was gonna marry me, then ask for a divorce and walk away with a bank account full of Cartwright oil money."

Amy clenched her hands, wishing her fingers were wrapped around the Kayla woman's neck.

"I can't seem to find a lady who wants just me, Lil. Not my money. Or my name. Me, damn it."

"Naughty."

"Yeah, that was another naughty word. Don't say it, okay?"

"'Kay."

"I want a woman who can stand on her own two feet."

"'Kay."

"If any woman needs rescuing, Lil, it's your mama."

Eyes burning, Amy retreated to the front door. She'd been rescued once in her life by a cowboy who'd done the right thing and married her and that sure as heck hadn't panned out.

One way or another she'd show Matt Cartwright that she didn't require his white-knight services.

THE RHYTHMIC CREAKING of the porch swing woke Amy around midnight. She sat up on the couch and rubbed her eyes, then headed into the kitchen, pausing at the screen door. Matt sat on the swing, his injured leg stretched out before him on the seat.

They hadn't said more than a few words to each other all evening. After warming up a plate of chicken casserole for him, she'd bathed the girls and tucked them into bed. Then she'd taken a shower and made up the couch, insisting Matt sleep upstairs where he'd be more comfortable. He'd put up a token fuss, but fell asleep before she'd left the room.

She pushed open the screen door and stepped outside. The swing stopped moving. "Leg hurt?" she asked.

"A little."

"Should I get the Naproxen?"

"I took a few pills a half hour ago." He slid his injured leg off the seat and patted the space next to him.

She shouldn't. But she did. As soon as she sat, Matt put the swing in motion and the sweet scent of lilac from the blooming bushes surrounding the porch engulfed her. For a few minutes the sound of croaking frogs and chirping crickets serenaded them.

"I'm sorry," Amy confessed.

"For what?" He brushed a curl from her cheek and his gentle touch almost drowned out her guilt.

"SOS hurting you was my fault." At his frown she sucked in a deep breath and explained. "A couple of months before Christmas, Rose asked for a dog." Amy remembered the moment as if it had happened yesterday.

As soon as her daughter had hopped into the truck after getting off the school bus… *Mama, Butch got a new puppy and brought it for show-and-tell*. Amy had made the appropriate murmurs and laughed when Rose described the puppy's antics in the classroom.

Can we get a puppy, Mama? Please?

"I didn't have the heart to tell Rose we didn't have the money for a pet. I said I'd think about it." Amy regretted the way she'd handled the situation. She shouldn't have given Rose false hope. "Every week she asked for a puppy and I made up excuses off the top of my head." Then her daughter had made her feel even worse. "Rose switched tactics and began talking about rescuing a dog from the shelter." The lump in Amy's throat swelled bigger, forcing her to swallow several times before she found her voice.

"I kept saying no. She finally stopped asking and I'd believed she'd forgotten all about it. If I'd known she'd been so desperate for a companion, that she'd adopt a barn rat, I would have found a way to get her a dog."

Matt's arm wrapped around her shoulder and she leaned in, accepting his hug. "It's my fault Ben died," she whispered.

"Oh, no, you don't." Matt took her by the arms. "Ben's death was not your fault. And it wasn't Rose's fault. I suspect at one time SOS was bitten by a rat and now the stud panics when he senses a rodent nearby."

"But if Rose hadn't been feeding the rat then—"

"Then nothing, Amy. Sophia had probably lived in

the barn for a long time. She would have come out in the open eventually whether Rose had fed her or not. It was sheer coincidence the rat appeared when Ben was in the stall with SOS."

Amy yearned to accept Matt's explanation. His fingers wiped at the tear tracks on her cheeks, then before she realized his intent, he kissed her—not a simple I-hope-you-feel-better kiss. But an *I-want-you kiss.*

More than willing to accept the distraction, Amy wound her arms around his neck and snuggled herself against him, soaking up the comfort he offered. The kiss became more passionate—mouths opened, tongues explored, sighs mingled. Matt's hand found her breast and she pushed against his fingers, dying for the feel of his callused palm against her bare flesh. He read her mind and snuck his hand beneath her nightshirt.

"I want you," he whispered, his fingers doing wicked things to her breast.

Matt's touch eased Amy's guilt—if only for a short time. "I want you, too."

Be careful you don't get burned, a voice inside her head warned.

Burned? Not possible when she knew exactly where Matt stood—opposite her. Making love with him would be an exercise in pure pleasure—nothing more. No commitment. No future. No expectations save for the here and now.

"Are you sure?" No man had ever gazed at her with such desire in his eyes.

"More than sure."

Chapter Eleven

Matt broke off their kiss and twirled one of Amy's bouncy curls around his finger. "As much as I'd like to make love to you on this swing, my leg won't cooperate." He stood and held out his hand. The glow of the full moon reflected off Amy's face and the warmth he read in her eyes brought him back for another kiss.

Pressing his lips to hers, he hoped to reassure himself that making love wouldn't change things between them. There was one certainty Matt clung to—he was going back to Oklahoma when the mares became pregnant. The rest was up for grabs.

"Everything will be all right," he whispered, wondering if the words were meant to reassure him or her. As their tongues mated, Matt concentrated on blocking out the voice in his head that was hell-bent on instigating a fight with his conscience.

Amy wouldn't make love to you if she knew you'd coaxed Ben into the card game.

She's sleeping with you because you paid her mortgage, bought groceries and babysat the girls until she found a sitter.

Matt prayed Amy's decision to make love with him wasn't grounded in gratitude. He wanted her to want *him*. To desire *him*. He was tempted to crawl out on a limb and confess his feelings, but no decent poker player showed his hand first.

He danced Amy toward the door, then ended the kiss.

"Last chance." He nuzzled her temple, breathing in the sweet scent of freshly washed hair. "No turning back once we're inside."

The pad of her thumb brushed his chin. "Maybe you're having second thoughts?"

Damn. What happened to his poker face? Was the turmoil gnawing his gut that obvious? Shoot, Amy was a widow. A mother. And a woman struggling to make it on her own. Any of those things was reason enough to keep his pants zipped.

He struggled to believe his helping Amy for a couple of months while he got what he wanted—stud service for his mares—would make amends for taking advantage of Ben. But Matt wasn't such a jerk that he didn't admit Amy, Wild Rose and Lily Pad had worked their way into his heart these past few weeks.

"I'm sure about one thing, Amy. You." He took her mouth, passion overriding lingering doubts and self-recrimination. He had one objective—to get this woman upstairs in bed. With him.

As soon as they entered the kitchen, Matt reached for the hem of her nightshirt and lifted the material over her head. Her bare breasts begged for his hands and mouth. They made it as far as the hall bath before he had Amy up against the wall. Her lush breasts filled his hands as he bent to taste them.

Her fingers sifting through Matt's hair, Amy's sighs filled his ears. Encouraged by her sensuous squirming, he snuck his hands beneath the elastic of her panties and cupped her smooth, bare bottom, bringing her firmly against his erection.

Their breathing ragged Matt decided he couldn't wait any longer and pressed Amy against the wall. When she lifted her leg and rested her knee on his hip, he teased the moist curls between her thighs. His mouth on her breasts, Amy bucked, her movements erratic. Determined she reach fulfillment, Matt dropped to one knee, ignoring the pain that shot through his injured thigh.

"Matt what… What are you… Oh…"

While his hands caressed her breasts, his mouth and tongue coaxed Amy higher. A few moments later, her head thunked the wall and a moan erupted from her mouth. Her legs folded and she slid down the wall until her bare fanny bumped the floor. Her breath puffed against his neck. "Matt…I… Holy cow…"

After a lingering kiss, he said, "Help me get to my feet."

Amy wiggled into her panties, then scooted out from beneath Matt. She steadied him as he braced his hands against the wall and pushed himself upright. His leg throbbed, but then so did another part of his body. "Here." He removed his T-shirt and tugged it over her head. "In case the girls wake up." He had a feeling the trek upstairs wouldn't be stealthlike.

They paused three times on the steps to exchange kisses, then again on the landing. Amy's hands were all over him—not that he was complaining but, it made traveling to their final destination time-consuming.

Once inside the bedroom, he shut the door and Amy flipped the lock. In a matter of seconds she had his zipper open. "I know you're thinking I'm a horny widow." She shoved his jeans over his hips, exposing his erection.

"You don't hear me complaining."

"Mmm," she murmured, her fingers sliding inside his briefs. This time *his* skull thunked the door.

A few more strokes and she sorely tested Matt's control. He shucked out of the rest of his clothes and Amy kicked free of hers. Matt's T-shirt landed on the other side of the room, along with her panties. Naked at last, they stared, eyes devouring. When Amy licked her lips, Matt growled.

He backed her up until her calves bumped the mattress, then she reclined on top of the bedspread, tugging Matt along. He rested his sore leg across her hips, which brought their lower bodies into perfect alignment.

"You're beautiful, Amy." A swath of pink exploded across her cheeks and Matt peppered the trail with kisses.

"You don't have to say that," she protested. "I know what I am—a plain Jane."

"Plain gorgeous." He trailed a finger along the faint blue vein bisecting her throat. "Your breasts are sexy and full and they make me want to bury my face in them."

Arching, she invited him closer. He nuzzled the soft swells, inhaling her tantalizing scent before feasting on the bountiful treasure.

"My turn." She rocked against him, her fingers toying with his nipples.

On the brink of losing it, he pulled Amy beneath him. "I want to be inside you." He snatched his wallet from the nightstand and found a condom inside it. Amy helped sheath him and then he forgot everything and everyone but her. He wanted to confess how much he liked her. Admired her. But feared he'd bungle the words. Instead he used his body to show her.

Amy revealed a playful side, tickling a chuckle out of him one second, then taunting him with seductive whispers the next. She told him how handsome he was. How sexy she found his body. He'd heard the same words from other women, but only Amy's opinion mattered. The truth was in her brown eyes and he basked in her approval.

"No one's ever made me feel the way you do," she sighed in his ear.

Moved by her confession, he kissed her gently. Amy was his here and now. For the moment—his world. She wrapped her legs around his waist and he slid inside her. Mouths fused, he mimicked the movement of his lower body with his tongue. Time passed in an erotic haze of sensation. A blur of spikes and dips, culminating in a spiraling ascent, which propelled them into a world where the past was forgotten and only the future existed.

AT 3:00 A.M. SUNDAY MORNING, Amy awoke to find herself snuggled against Matt's warm body. She brushed her finger against his six-pack, then nudged his groin with her knee. *Perfect.*

His snores tickled her ears and she smiled, rubbing her cheek over his smooth chest. The poor cowboy was tuckered out. Matt was so much more than she'd first assumed when he'd shown up at the farm. And the possessive heat in his eyes when he'd slid inside her had captured her heart. Yep, she'd fallen head over heels for another cowboy. And this time it wasn't a youthful crush.

This time it was love.

Matt might be a cowboy, but he was honest and decent and good with her daughters. Amy closed her eyes and pictured the four of them as a family raising horses on the farm, spending her days and nights with Matt at her side.

He made her feel feminine and beautiful—as if the eight extra pounds she'd struggled to shed the past two years had only added to her attractiveness. The rodeo cowboy had his pick of women—the fact that little ol' her turned his head darn near intoxicated her.

Don't become too smug. The voice in her head reminded her of the woman she'd overheard Matt discussing with Lily in the bathroom not long ago. Kayla had broken Matt's heart, leaving Amy to wonder if he'd ever allow himself to love another woman. Was it possible to coax Matt into risking his heart again? Did she dare try?

Amy struggled to come up with a list of things she and Matt had in common besides a love of horses. After little success she composed a mental tally of things they didn't have in common.

He was rich—she was barely scraping by.

He was famous—she was…well, Amy. Plain ol' Amy.

He had no children—she had two daughters.

He regarded the glass of life half-full—she viewed it half-empty.

He had big plans for his horse-breeding operation—she wanted a little piece of security for her and the girls.

Everything about Matt was bolder and bigger—right down to his sexy smile. He popped against the canvas of life whereas she blended into the background.

Matt's energy and optimistic attitude made her wish to step out of her comfort zone and lay everything— even her heart—on the line for him. But their lives were headed in different directions—his to Oklahoma and hers right here on the farm. Watching Matt drive away at the end of the summer would be difficult even if her heart hadn't taken a nosedive for him.

"I can hear your brain thinking." His voice rumbled across the top of her head.

Smiling, she brushed her fingertips over his abdomen. She shifted in order to see his face, then sucked in a quiet breath at the tight lines bracketing his mouth. "Your leg is hurting, isn't it?" She popped off the bed and snatched her bathrobe from the hook on the inside of the closet door. "I'll get the pain medicine." That he didn't protest verified her suspicion. She hurried to the kitchen, poured a glass of iced tea and grabbed the bottle of Naproxen.

"Here." She placed the pills and the tea on the nightstand, then helped Matt sit up. "What are you smiling about?" she asked when he grinned.

He waggled his eyebrows at the front of her robe where her breasts threatened to spill out. "Stop that," she scolded, tightening the belt before she brushed at a strand of his mussed hair.

"You're incredible." He caught her hand and brought her fingers to his lips.

Knees weak, she sank to the edge of the mattress. Her conscience insisted it was okay to love this man. Here in her room she could be what she wanted. Do what she wanted. Dream what she wanted—that all her tomorrows included Matt. As long as she understood that the moment she left the bedroom her world would revert to normal. And normal meant that one day soon Matt would leave her behind.

She offered her mouth. Matt took it. Their kiss was soft and gentle. "Come to bed with me," he whispered, then coaxed her tongue into dueling with his. Unable to refuse him anything—even for his own good—she slipped out of her robe. His hand clutched her naked hip, then curved around her waist…over her bottom… along her thigh. His callused fingers tickled the sensitive skin behind her knee before traveling to the front of her thigh and inching upward…inward.

Her nipples hardened and her head fell forward as she basked in his caresses. Then Matt moved the covers aside, sat on the edge of the bed and pulled her between his thighs. So what if he wouldn't allow himself to fall in love again? Amy was positive she wasn't merely another notch in the cowboy's championship belt. She yearned to confess her love, but settled for conveying her feelings through sighs of pleasure.

Carefully, she straddled his lap, his erection nudging her heat. "All I want is to be with you," he whispered. "Around you. In you."

She grabbed the words and tucked them into the corner of her heart. Words would have to be enough. For now. Forever.

He sheathed himself, then they took off again on another journey where Amy played make-believe with her and Matt's future.

MATT'S SLEEP-FOGGED BRAIN woke in bits and pieces. He resisted opening his eyes; instead he fantasized about Amy and the incredible night he'd spent with her. He'd been so sure that he had a handle on his feelings for the woman, but after making love with her, holding her…he was out of his ever-loving mind if he believed he'd drive off into the sunset without a worry in the world once the mares conceived.

Right now the idea of walking away from Amy left a bad taste in his mouth that had nothing to do with needing to brush his teeth. Why was he attracted to a woman who didn't have her act together? Who struggled with bad luck and bad times? Who wanted his help, not him?

He slid his leg sideways, enjoying the feel of the cool sheet against his skin. The light behind his closed eyelids told him that it was way past rise-'n'-shine time. A part of him wanted to remain in bed and not face Amy. Would she fantasize that their lovemaking was equivalent to their own happy ever after? He hoped not. After mulling it over, he decided he'd better concentrate on SOS and his mares. From now on he'd stick to business—horse business. He cracked an eye open, surprised to discover he wasn't alone in the room.

"Are you gonna sleep all day?" Two little flower buds peered at him from the end of the bed.

Lily moved closer and set her rubber duck on his chest. "Duck."

"Thanks, Lil." He glanced at Rose. "Where's your mom?"

"Outside feeding the horses."

Today was Sunday. Enough lazing around in bed. He swung his legs off the side of the mattress, making sure the blanket concealed his naked state. "You girls go outside and play while I take a shower."

"Mama said we gotta babysit you."

Suspicious, he asked, "How long have you been watching me sleep?"

"Forever." Rose clicked the button on the walkie-talkie. "Mama, Mr. Matt's awake. Over."

"Tell Mr. Matt I'll come up to the house in a minute."

Matt motioned for the radio. "Mornin', darlin'."

"How are you feeling? Over." She sounded all businesslike.

"Lonely. Want to come inside and keep me company? Over."

After a long pause... "Amy's busy feedin' the horses, but I'd be happy to keep you company. Over."

Matt's face flamed. "Hey, Jake. Over."

"Heard about your leg. Stopped by to help Amy with the horses. Over."

"I appreciate that. Over."

"No problem. Best be on my way now." Jake was silent for a moment, then said, "Amy explained about the rat."

Matt quickly covered the speaker with his hand, but Rose's gape confirmed he hadn't been quick enough. "Gotta go. Over." He turned off the walkie-talkie.

"What happened to Sophia?" Tears pooled in Rose's eyes.

Refusing to have this conversation half-naked, he insisted, "Wait downstairs. I'll explain everything after I put some clothes on."

"You killed her, didn't you!" Rose fled the room.

"Lily, go with your sister." As soon as the toddler left, Matt tossed on the T-shirt and jeans he'd worn yesterday, then hurried after the girls. He entered the kitchen as Amy walked in from the porch. She froze when she spotted him and immediately his mind recalled her naked body sprawled across his. He shook his head to dispel the picture and concentrated on the crisis at hand. "Where's Rose?"

"She's not in here with you?" Amy fled outside, taking the porch steps two at a time.

Unable to keep up, Matt trailed behind, wincing at the pull of sore muscles. He hobbled around to the side of the house where he found Amy attempting to coax her daughter from the playhouse. Ignoring her sister's sobs, Lily chased a butterfly in the garden.

"Let me talk to Rose." He sent Amy a silent message. *This is between Rose and me. You aren't supposed to know, remember?*

With a nod, Amy coaxed Lily inside the house. Rose's sniffles tugged at his heart. The Olson females had sure had their share of misery lately. "Can I come in?" he asked.

"Yeah."

Matt opened the miniature door and crawled inside, leaving the lower half of his body lying outside the house. What to do—fib or tell the truth? Neither choice held much appeal. He settled for a little bit of both. "Yesterday Sophia left the tack room and snuck into SOS's stall."

The little girl's dainty chin rose. "Didn't you feed her?"

"I fed her." Shoot, he'd tried using Amy's leftover casserole to coax the rat into the trap, but the rodent wouldn't touch the stuff. "I guess I didn't feed her enough because she went searching for more food."

Rose hiccupped. "What happened to her?"

"She got caught under SOS's hooves." He spared her the gory details.

"Did she cry?"

"Nope. Not a peep out of her. It happened so fast she didn't feel a thing, honey."

Rose rubbed her hand across her runny nose. "Can I see her?" She must have sensed he was about to protest because she begged, "Please."

"Sure. But not right now. I'll make a little box to put her in, then you can decide where to bury her."

The child responded with a shuddering sigh.

"I'm sorry, honey. I know you and Sophia were good friends."

Right then the child launched herself at Matt, flinging her arms around his neck. She wailed against the front of his shirt and he held her gently. "Don't cry, baby. Please, don't cry."

Her sobs grew in strength and Matt was desperate to stop the tears. "Tomorrow we'll go adopt a puppy," he blurted.

Rose lifted her head and rubbed her watery eyes. "I can have a dog?"

Shit. What had he gone and done now? "Yes, you can have a dog." *If I'm able to talk your mother into it.*

The tears dried up. "Promise?"

"Promise."

"I'm gonna tell Mama and Lily!" She scrambled across Matt's body and dashed to the house.

Matt stayed behind. No sense crawling out. As soon as Amy discovered what he'd done, he'd be in the dog house anyway.

Chapter Twelve

Late Friday afternoon Amy sat in her truck outside United Savings and Loan in Pebble Creek and studied the fake fern hanging in the bank window.

Almost a week had passed since she and Matt had made love—five days and not a single kiss or accidental brushing of hands. Nothing but one-word answers and glances that pinged off Amy like hail on a tin roof.

At first she'd been embarrassed by Matt's disinterest in her and guessed he hadn't enjoyed the sex as much as she had. But after a lengthy analysis of their lovemaking, she'd concluded—based on groans, grunts and overall enthusiasm—that Matt had had a real good time with her between the sheets.

Next, she'd felt hurt…she was a female after all and a little reassurance—a smile, a compliment, a kind word that after giving birth to two babies and burying a husband she still appealed to the opposite sex— would have been appreciated.

Anger followed the hurt. She'd been—still was— mad at herself for assuming that making love would change things between her and Matt. She was a big girl capable of engaging in a summer fling without allowing her emotions to tangle the experience, but Matt had worked his way under her skin in such a short time that making love with him had landed a knockout punch to her heart.

Was it merely three weeks ago that she'd been convinced Matt was simply another sexy cowboy with big dreams? In no time flat he'd proved her wrong. Matt Cartwright was one of the good guys. Her heart recognized the fact and she'd fallen in love with him.

Matt was more than a successful rodeo cowboy. He was levelheaded, responsible, prideful, determined and kind-hearted—he had a soft spot for the girls and that lug of a dog he'd brought home from the animal shelter this past Monday. And his attributes didn't stop there. He was patient and caring—what man in his right mind would play nanny to two kids, one not yet potty-trained?

For the life of her, Amy couldn't figure out Matt's avoidance issues and feared his sudden cold feet was the result of the stupid woman from his past who'd set her sights on his money and in the end had broken his heart. Why was Matt unable to see that she was different? More than ever Amy wished he'd never made her mortgage payments. Wished he hadn't bought all those groceries.

Her gaze slid to the envelope resting beside her on the seat. She conceded she might have come off as a bit desperate, but that was before she'd finally dug out her father's notebook. Agitated by the turn her relationship with Matt had taken, Amy had put her sleepless nights to good use reading her father's get-rich-quick journal. Her father had been a schemer and a dreamer like Ben. Sadly, both men had died before either had realized their dreams.

Ben had missed out on the chance to see SOS's stud fees solve their monetary problems, and her father had never had the opportunity to capitalize on the discovery he'd made shortly before his death—the Broken Wheel was sitting on a fortune in phosphate, a mineral used in the production of fertilizer and other chemicals. Amy suspected Payton Scott knew about the phosphate and that's why he was pressuring her to sell—because he intended to be first in line with an offer as soon as the For Sale sign went up in her yard.

Although eager to share her discovery with Matt, Amy decided to wait for the results of a geological survey to validate her father's claim. Once she had proof she wasn't after Matt's money, she'd turn her attention to wooing the cowboy for the remainder of the summer. By the time Rose started school at the end of August Matt would have more reasons to stay than to leave.

First things first. She intended to give Payton a piece of her mind and then some. "Hi, Shelly," Amy greeted the receptionist when she entered the bank lobby. "Is Payton in?"

Shelly smacked her gum and nodded, never taking her eyes off the computer screen in front of her. Amy padded across the carpet and waltzed into Payton's office unannounced. The girlie magazine his face was buried in flew across the desk, knocking over the pencil tin and an empty soda can. He grabbed the

magazine and stuffed it into a drawer. Red-faced, he
sputtered, "What do you want?"

"About the mortgage payment—"

"Let me guess. You can't make the next one?" He
leered. "Ready to sell?"

Dream on. "I came to inform you that I landed a job
with Vista Insurance."

Payton's blubbery lips parted, but no words escaped
his mouth.

In case he thought she was yanking his pant leg, she
pulled the company brochure from her purse and
tossed it his way. "My data-entry class ends next
Friday and the following Monday I'll begin working
from home for Vista." The company promised to
deliver and install a computer in her house, enabling
her to input insurance claims using the company
software program. The job came with health insurance
for her and the girls, as well as paid sick leave and
vacation time after six months. Her professor had
heard about the job opening and considered Amy a
good candidate for the position, so he'd arranged an
interview for her this past Wednesday after class.

"Part-time work, Amy?" Payton snickered.

She wanted to slam his head against the desk. "Full-
time." She was allowed to work as many hours a week
as she wished, but the company didn't offer overtime
pay.

"What are they giving you an hour?"

"Ten dollars."

His sleet-colored eyes widened. "You'll never make
it on sixteen hundred dollars a month, and that's before
taxes and social security are taken out of your paycheck."

"Don't forget, Payton, I'll be boarding horses on the side, as well."

He snorted. "Heard about Cartwright's kick in the ass from that renegade stallion in your barn."

"He got kicked in the *thigh*." She didn't owe the banker any explanation, but hoped to spread the word that SOS wasn't to blame for Ben's death. "Matt discovered what sets SOS off—rats."

"Ben died because of a rat?"

Amy harbored a small measure of guilt for her husband's senseless death. Who knew what might have happened if she'd allowed Rose to have a puppy.

Payton chuckled, the sound reminiscent of a cackling witch. "Good luck finding a buyer who has a rat-free barn."

She'd have her work cut out locating someone willing to take on the stud's phobia. But keeping the stallion wasn't an option. Once her debts were paid off, the salary from her job with Vista Insurance plus the income from boarding horses—providing her customers returned— would cover the mortgage payment and monthly bills. She wouldn't be living high off the hog, but she'd keep her farm. Worst-case scenario—she'd sell a portion of the land's mineral rights and pay off the mortgage in full.

Time to drop the bomb and wipe that spit-slick grin off Payton's face. "Why did you allow Ben and me to take out a second mortgage on the farm if you knew Ben was a bad risk?" People across two counties were aware of her husband's gambling addiction.

"That was always part of the plan, Amy." He crossed his arms behind his head, the movement lifting his pudgy paunch higher.

"By plan, I presume you mean this." She held up the document from the land surveyor her father had hired.

Payton shot forward in the chair. "What's that?"

"A letter confirming the presence of the mineral phosphate on the farm. I suspect you know this already and that's why you're after my land." The surveyor suggested an in-depth geological study be conducted to confirm the amount and value, but her father had died and hadn't been able to pursue the next step.

Beads of sweat bubbled across Payton's forehead. "Where did you get that? Your father kept all his personal papers in a bank deposit box."

"Yeah, funny how this letter was missing when I collected his things after he died. Lucky for me he'd kept the original at home." In his black notebook.

"If you don't pay your July mortgage on time, I'll foreclose on you so fast your head will spin," Payton growled.

"As long as I have breath in me, you'll never get your hands on my farm." Enough said. She stormed out of the bank.

Amy hopped into her truck and clenched the steering wheel until her knuckles ached. Payton Scott was no better than a playground bully. Granted discovering the presence of phosphate on the farm would, she hoped, provide long-term security for her and the girls, but it did nothing to help her current dilemma. Where was she going to come up with sixteen hundred dollars by July?

Matt.

If she asked him to bail her out again, he'd believe she was no better than that hussy Kayla. Amy's back was to the wall. She didn't dare tell Matt about the phosphate discovery until the geologist from the Idaho Geological Survey had a chance to conduct a series of soil tests. If the results confirmed what her father had believed all along, then she'd have proof she possessed the means to pay Matt back.

Shoving aside her money woes, Amy headed home. For the first time in a long while hope blossomed in her. Tonight she wished to celebrate—maybe go out for pizza in Rockton. Later, after she tucked the girls into bed, she'd gather her courage and ask Matt for another loan.

The big question was…before or after she set out to seduce him?

MATT STOOD OUTSIDE SOS'S STALL and watched Nathan examine the stallion. Not long ago he'd witnessed the stud wooing Cinnamon in the pasture and had asked Nathan to stop by to see if the mare had become pregnant—she hadn't. Mother Nature refused to be rushed, but it would be better for everyone—mainly him and Amy—if the process didn't take the entire summer.

Making love to Amy had been more than great sex. The way her eyes had softened as he slid inside her had captured his heart and made him yearn to tuck her against his side and protect her forever. But what rattled him most about Amy was the knowledge that she loved him. No, she hadn't said the words out loud, but her love shone in each smile, each look she gave him.

That softness in her eyes was the reason Matt had to leave.

He couldn't live with himself if Amy found out the truth about the poker game in Pocatello. Any love she held for Matt would die an instant death when she discovered he'd lured Ben into a card game for Matt's own personal gain.

Hoping to spare his heart a death blow, he'd decided the best course of action was to keep his pants zipped and steer clear of Amy. Avoiding the woman had been a bigger challenge than roping a recalcitrant rodeo calf. Each time their eyes connected the smoky message in her gaze whispered *make love to me.*

"Am I jumping the gun?" Matt asked the vet, forcing his brain to focus on the business at hand.

"Maybe. Maybe not." The tall, lanky veterinarian with bushy red hair drew blood from the stallion's neck. SOS gave no indication he was agitated or nervous. The horse understood Sophia was no longer a threat. To be on the safe side, Matt had set out a handful of traps, daring any rodent to enter the barn.

Nathan stowed the blood sample in his medical bag, then palpated the stallion's testes. "How recent was his last sire?"

"A year ago this past spring." Matt had come across information on SOS when he'd researched studs for his mares. The animal's list of offspring had been impressive.

"When did Ben purchase him?"

"Not sure. Late November or early December of last year."

"Were vet records included in the stallion's paperwork?"

"Not that I know of." Nathan's mouth twisted and Matt's gut clenched. "What is it?"

"One of his testicles is smaller than the other." Nathan stepped from the stall, latched the door.

"Which means…?" Matt prompted.

"He might have suffered a kick from a mare while trying to mount, or contracted a viral infection that settled in one of the testes."

"I haven't noticed any swelling—"

"The injury would have occurred months ago—before Ben purchased the horse."

"Will a smaller testicle prevent SOS from impregnating a mare?"

"Before we jump to conclusions, we'll send off his sperm for analysis."

"Can you collect a sample today?"

"If you'd like. Is there a phantom mare around?"

"In the tack room." Matt had come across the man-made mount when he'd cleaned the barn. A phantom mare was used for a variety of reasons—to give young, inexperienced stallions practice in mounting techniques so they wouldn't hurt the mares. To increase a stallion's sperm count by allowing the horse to mount regularly. And to enable breeders to collect sperm samples.

"I'll set up the mount in the barn." With luck he and Nathan would finish with SOS before Amy left Rockton. He hoped to spare her any worry—as if she didn't already have enough to fret over.

Part of Matt hoped the stallion proved healthy, which would enable Amy to sell the animal and pay off her debts. The other part of him hoped SOS was shooting blanks.

Then Matt would have no reason to stay.

As Amy drove up to the house she spotted the local vet's rig. All three mares were in the corral. Matt must have called Nathan about SOS. She hoped it was nothing serious. She wanted Matt in a good mood tonight when she seduced him—that is, if she figured out how. Her previous attempts had netted little success.

She parked the truck, then headed for the barn, but stopped at the sound of a loud *woof.* Moose, as he'd been affectionately called at the animal shelter, loped across the yard, his sagging jowls swaying side-to-side like a Hawaiian honey in a hula skirt.

At first, she'd been angry at Matt for overstepping his bounds with Rose, but Amy's guilt had gotten the best of her—if she'd allowed her daughter to have a dog months ago Ben might be alive today. In the end she'd agreed to a dog on one condition—that it wasn't a snippy little yapping house mutt. She wanted an outside dog and one that didn't act up around the horses.

Well, she'd gotten her wish, but she hadn't been expecting a mastiff. Moose was one hundred and ten pounds of drooling affection. His dark face and jowls stood out against his wheat-colored body. At first Amy had feared the dog would play too rough with the girls, but after watching the trio romp around the yard, it was obvious Moose was a gentle giant. Lily pulled, pinched and prodded, but the dog took it all in stride as if they were love pats.

The shelter had told Matt that Moose had been dropped off when his master, a soldier in the Army Reserve, had been called up to duty and was unable to find a home for the animal before he shipped out.

Even though the dog was good with the girls, Amy wasn't sold on Moose until she'd watched Matt introduce him to the horses. Moose showed little interest in the mares or SOS and didn't bark once at the horses—probably because it took too much energy. The dog was the laziest animal she'd ever seen. All he did was lounge in the sun on the porch, then move to the shade beneath the tree in the yard as the day grew warmer. And when she and the girls were inside, Moose sat by the door, his drooling jowls smashed against the screen, watching them eat.

Rose took over the duty of feeding the dog three small meals a day—to avoid bloat according to the shelter employees. Amy imagined the stink from a dog that size when it let one rip. His first night on the farm Amy had allowed Moose in the house because she hadn't been able to shut the door on the animal's pathetic droopy-eyed face. Moose had followed the girls upstairs and had stretched out in the hallway outside their door. All was well until the dog began to snore and wheeze, keeping Amy up all night. These days Moose slept on an old couch cushion on the porch.

"Hi, Amy!" Nicole walked out of the house with Lily on her hip, Rose trailing behind. Today had been her eldest daughter's last day of first grade.

Amy called for Moose to follow and she hurried to greet the girls. After hugs and kisses she spoke to the sitter. "How'd everything go?"

"Fine." Nicole glanced at her watch. "You're home early."

"The exam didn't take long." Amy dug inside her purse for a twenty-dollar bill. "Thank you so much for watching the girls."

"Rose and Lily are no trouble at all. But Moose is a big baby."

Lily pointed to the dog. "Me, Moo."

Nicole set Lily on her feet and Amy's daughter launched herself at the dog, squeezing his neck and burying her face against his slobbery jowls. Not only had Moose's smell permeated Amy's house, but now her girls reeked like dog, too.

"See you again Monday." Nicole headed to her car.

"Bye, Nicole!" Rose shouted as the babysitter drove off.

"What's wrong with SOS?" Amy asked her daughter.

"I don't know." Rose patted her leg. "Come, Moose. Supper." The dog trotted after his little masters.

Amy cast a longing glance toward the barn before following the trio inside.

HE CAN'T AVOID YOU FOREVER.

Amy fidgeted in the kitchen, shoring up the nerve to seek Matt out in the barn. How many times a day did she find herself gazing through the glass panes hoping for a glimpse of the cowboy?

Nathan had driven away late that afternoon. Suppertime had come and gone. She'd rung the bell on the porch to signal dinner was on the table, but Matt had skipped joining them. No surprise. He hadn't eaten with her and the girls all week. An hour ago she'd tucked the girls into bed, then grabbed a quick shower and changed into a cotton sundress.

A sudden burning sensation in her eyes caught her off guard and she mumbled an unladylike curse. She was supposed to be celebrating, not simpering like a fool. As soon as her eyes stopped watering she'd confront Matt and demand an explanation for his aloofness. If Matt had learned anything about her the past month, then he'd know she wasn't a quitter. She wasn't giving him —thcm—up without a fight.

A shadow stepped from the barn and Amy held her breath as Matt headed toward the house. A short time later his boots hit the porch steps. Next came the squeak of the screen door. Then a quiet woof from Moose, who'd been sleeping on his cushion.

"Hey, Moose. Keeping an eye on my girls?"

The note of affection in Matt's voice twisted Amy's heart. Whether he wanted to admit it or not, he cared about her, Rose and Lily. "Hi, Matt."

He stiffened, his head swinging her way. "Thought you'd all gone to bed."

She'd assumed as much. Amy had flipped off the lights earlier, not wanting him to spot her silhouette in the window. His scent—male sweat, horse and a hint of the aftershave sitting on the bathroom sink reached her nose and she breathed deeply. "I noticed Nathan stopped by today."

"Nothing to worry about."

His clipped response sent up red flags in her head. "Why did he—"

"Let me grab a quick shower and we'll talk." Then he was gone, leaving Amy in the dark once again.

Chapter Thirteen

Matt, dressed in a clean pair of jeans and a T-shirt, padded barefoot down the hall. He stopped at the top of the stairs and ran his fingers through his hair. He expected two questions from Amy when he entered the kitchen: why the vet had paid a visit today and why Matt was avoiding her. He wasn't eager to answer either inquiry. He gave himself a mental shove, descended the stairs and found Amy where he'd left her— in front of the window, staring at the darkening sky.

Had it been three weeks since he'd arrived at the farm with his mares in tow? Funny how time had slowed to a crawl, each day feeling longer than the previous. He'd become so comfortable interacting with Rose and Lily that the volunteer at the animal shelter had mistakenly believed the girls were his daughters.

Funny how you didn't bother to correct the woman.

He must have made a sound because Amy spun and offered him that sweet, sexy smile she'd flashed on and off all week. Enough light from the hall spilled into the room, enabling him to read the anxiety in her brown eyes.

Right then he cursed himself for making love to her and stirring things up between them. They should have kept their relationship professional or at most, friends. But they'd crossed the line and become lovers and Matt had fallen hard for the widow.

Amy didn't have to do much to trigger a physical response from him. A look. A smile. A sigh. And he was ready. Right now, he ached to take her in his arms and replace the uncertainty in her gaze with the sated, relaxed smile she wore after making love.

She hadn't uttered a single word, but her eyes urged him closer. He stopped inches in front of her, wrapped a finger around a soft curl and tugged gently, bringing her face forward. The tiny catch in her throat shot straight to his groin and he used his mouth to show her how much he'd missed her this week. Missed touching her. Missed her scent…her softness.

He meant only to kiss her, but his hand found her breast. She wasn't wearing a bra. He slid the dress off her shoulders and stared. She made an erotic picture, standing before him bare-chested with her dress pooling at her waist. He lowered his mouth to her nipple…teased. Tormented. Licked and nibbled.

Fingers threading through his hair, she confessed, "I've missed you."

The three little words blew his good intentions— what there had been of them anyway—to smithereens. Nothing mattered but making love to Amy. Hands and mouths collided. His T-shirt landed on the floor. He set her on the counter and stood between her legs. The sound of ragged breathing echoed seductively around them.

"What about your leg?" she whispered, caressing his denim-covered thigh.

"The leg is fine." He shifted her hand to the bulge at the front of his jeans. "This hurts."

Giggling, she said, "I can help with that." Then she lowered the zipper and together they shoved his jeans past his hips. He flipped her dress up around her waist and groaned.

"You're not wearing any panties." His fingers stroked the moist curls.

"I was hoping…" She sighed the words into his mouth.

Amy had planned to seduce him tonight? *Lucky man.* No more words were spoken. She found the condom in his wallet and sheathed him, then he thrust inside her. Their mating was hard and hot and neither wanted it to end. Then her fingernails dug into his shoulders and she buried her face in his neck and moaned her release. Matt was right behind her. Another thrust and he reached his own climax.

Amy wasn't sure how long her and Matt's bodies had remained tangled before her bottom went numb. She wiggled loose from his hold and in silence they helped one another adjust their clothes. Taking his hand she led him to the porch swing. Moose followed, resting on his cushion. Feeling lazy and loved, she curled against Matt's side. With his arm around her, Amy was prepared to face any challenge life threw her way. "What was Nathan doing here today?"

For a moment he stopped breathing.

Worried, she asked, "Is something the matter with SOS?"

"Everything's fine. I haven't had the mares long so I'm not familiar with their cycles. Nathan checked to see which are in estrus."

"And?"

"Cinnamon's the only one."

Thank God. Amy hoped for a never-ending summer. Matt stared into space and Amy worried about his sudden aloofness. Deciding to change the subject she said, "Guess what?"

"What?"

"I got a job offer."

"You did?" He shifted toward her.

"Vista Insurance. I'm keying information on insurance forms into their company software program. The course instructor heard of the job and recommended me. I had an interview this past Wednesday and Vista offered me the job today."

"Congratulations." He bent his head to kiss her cheek, but she twisted at the last second, ensuring their lips bumped. This time the kiss wasn't hot or heavy, but soft and gentle. When it ended, Amy wanted more. She always wanted more. Matt was an exceptional kisser.

"A week from Monday the insurance company is delivering a computer to the house. This way I'll be able to work from home and won't have to pay for child care. Once I sell SOS, my regular customers will board their horses at the farm, then my worries are over."

"What do you mean?"

"Even if I don't get top dollar for SOS, the money he brings in will go a long way in paying off my debt. And my income from the insurance company combined with boarding horses should be enough to cover the mortgage and monthly expenses."

"You've got it all figured out," he mumbled.

"Well, sort of," she hedged. Gathering her courage… "I realize I owe you for both the May and June mortgage payments, but is it possible to borrow another sixteen hundred for July?"

When Matt didn't respond, she assured, "As soon as I receive my first full paycheck from Vista I'll begin reimbursing you."

"Sure." He sprang from the swing and moved to the porch steps. "I'll stop by the bank tomorrow and deposit the money into your account."

Why wasn't he making eye contact with her?

"Time to turn in," he said.

That's it? They weren't going to make love again? Her throat swelled. "Not feeling well?"

"Tired is all. 'Night." Then he was gone.

Leaving Amy feeling abandoned and downright ticked.

"WHATCHA DOIN'?" Rose asked when Matt stepped from the barn.

"How long have you been standing out here?"

Slim shoulders shrugged. "I don't know."

"Where's Lily?"

"Napping."

"Where's your mother?" Matt hungered for a glimpse of Amy.

Rose's chest filled with air, then she sighed dramatically. "Studying."

Today was Amy's last session of her data-entry

class. Seven days had passed since Matt and Amy's rendezvous in the kitchen. He'd managed to keep his hands to himself for the rest of the weekend, then Monday had arrived and everything had returned to normal—Amy left for Rockton in the afternoon and Nicole showed up to watch the girls. He'd hardly seen Amy all week—but out of sight did not mean out of mind. At least knowing she was busy with class work helped him control the urge to go up to the house and...*never mind* with her.

Wiggling the stick in her hand, Rose asked, "Want me to show you the trick I taught Moose?"

"Sure." Matt chuckled. The dog was dead to the world, snoozing on the porch. As he watched Rose dash off to coax Moose from his nap, Matt's chest tightened with emotion. He'd miss Amy's daughters when he left.

With a lot of prodding and a biscuit, Rose convinced the dog to follow her to the barn. "Watch this," she said.

Moose didn't budge as his droopy eyes followed the stick sailing through the air.

"Go get it, Moose. C'mon." Rose stomped her foot and grumbled, "Stupid dog."

Matt wasn't sure if he sympathized more with the kid or the dog. "Teaching Moose to fetch a stick is a lot like potty training Lily."

"Huh?" Rose wrinkled her nose.

"It takes time and patience. And you're going to have a few mess ups once in a while. Have you tried throwing him a ball?" When Rose shook her head, he said, "I put SOS out to pasture, so it's safe to come inside the barn." The little girl followed Matt past the empty horse stalls. "Let's see if there's a toy for Moose to play with in the storage room."

They rummaged through a trunk of junk and discovered a small rubber ball with a rope attached to it. Amy had probably hung the ball from a tree branch for the horses to play with while they grazed in pasture.

When they exited the barn, the dog grew excited and barked. Rose kicked the ball and Moose took off like a rocket. Rose's squeal of excitement died a quick death when the mastiff refused to bring the ball back, preferring to shove it around the ground with his face.

"He's a soccer player," Matt said.

Rose joined in the soccer game with Moose while Matt's eyes strayed to the house. He spotted Amy on the porch wearing a smile as she watched her daughter tussle with the dog. The breeze in the air stirred the curls around Amy's face and she repeatedly brushed strands of hair from her eyes. Then those beautiful brown eyes swung his way and even from a distance he read her mind...

What did I do wrong, Matt?

Not a damned thing, Amy.

Then why are you avoiding me?

Because I love you.

I love you, too.

You wouldn't if you knew the truth I've been keeping from you.

"Mama," Rose shouted. "Moose knows how to play soccer!"

Forced to focus on her daughter, Amy turned away

first. Matt disappeared inside the barn and spied from the shadows. When Amy discovered he'd walked off, she lowered her guard, closing her eyes and pinching the bridge of her nose between her fingertips.

Damn it, Amy, don't cry. Not over me.

After a moment she called for Rose to come inside for lunch. Moose remained behind, content to play with the ball alone. The sound of an approaching vehicle caught Matt's ear. Pebble Creek's veterinarian barreled up the drive. He hoped Nathan had good news.

"Matt," the vet greeted when he hopped out of the truck.

After the men shook hands, Matt got right to the point. "Any news from the lab?"

"They called this morning." Nathan's sober expression didn't bode well for the stud.

"And…?"

"For all intents and purposes, SOS's sperm count is so low he's considered sterile."

"Oh, hell." Matt shoved his fingers through his hair. Wait until Amy heard this latest bit of news.

"I'm sorry, Matt."

Sorry for what? For Ben being a stupid ass and not having a vet confirm the stallion's fertility before purchasing the animal? Sorry that the stud was of no use to Amy and now she had no means with which to pay off the debts her husband had saddled her with? Sorry Matt would have to drive back to Oklahoma with his tail tucked between his legs and confess his big plans to breed horses had backfired?

"Would you like me to break the news to Amy?" Nathan interrupted Matt's internal agonizing.

"No. I will." If Matt had his way, Amy would never learn SOS was sterile. "Thanks for driving out to deliver the news in person." Small-town hospitality at its best.

"Sure thing." Nathan tipped his hat, then hopped into his truck and sped off.

Numb with shock, Matt returned to the barn and sat on the hay bale in the corner. He attempted to summon up some anger, but the single emotion pulsing through him was relief—he finally had a legitimate reason to leave the Broken Wheel.

What was he going to tell Amy?

In truth, Matt believed Amy was nothing like Kayla. Amy would never accept money from him for SOS if she learned the stallion was sterile. But it would be better for both of them—okay, mostly him—if she believed Matt had left because he was convinced she was after his money.

Telling Amy the real reason he had to leave wasn't an option. He cringed when he imagined the disbelief and hurt on her face if he confessed how he'd used her husband for his own personal gain. And for what? Nobody had walked away from that poker game a winner.

There was one way to make amends to Amy and if he had to drop to his knees and beg his father for a loan, he would. Matt intended to pay Amy's mortgage through the rest of the summer and buy SOS from her. It was the least he could do. Then he'd load up the horses and his guilty conscience and make a mad dash to Oklahoma, leaving Amy and her daughters to make a fresh start in life.

Tonight he'd bring in the horses from the pasture

and pack his things. He wanted to be ready to leave at a minute's notice.

Matt didn't have to wait long. Saturday morning after breakfast Amy announced the girls wanted to introduce Moose to Jake and Helen. Once the taillights on Amy's truck disappeared, Matt hit the ground running.

"THINGS OKAY BETWEEN YOU and Matt?" Jake asked Amy as they waited for Helen and the girls to come out of the house.

Keeping her expression neutral, Amy fibbed, "Sure. Why?"

"Matt's a good man." Jake grinned. "You might do worse for a second husband."

Amy nudged the dirt with the tip of her boot. She didn't dare let on that she'd fantasized about her and Matt tying the knot. She'd love nothing more than for Rose and Lily to have a real father—a man who spent quality time with them. And she certainly wouldn't complain about having a husband who showed a little interest in her.

If only she knew what was eating at Matt... But there was nothing left to do or say until he decided to confess whatever was bothering him. The waiting was excruciating—this constant yearning inside her exhausting. It had been a struggle to study this past week with her mind drifting to Matt and their lovemaking.

"Matt has his own plans for the future," she said.

"He mentioned raisin' cuttin' horses. Your farm's big enough for a small herd."

"His father owns a huge ranch, Jake."

"That might be, but you and the girls aren't in Oklahoma, are you?"

"It's not like that between us." At least not yet.

Jake expelled a grumpy *umph*. "Well, it ought to be if he's climbin' into your sleepin' bag at night."

Amy had nothing to say to that.

"Do you love him?"

She wanted to tell Jake to mind his own business, but didn't. He and Helen had stood by her side at the funeral home, when her own husband hadn't bothered to come in off the circuit for his in-laws' burial. Helen had prepared all the food for the visitation at the house following the church service. Jake had looked after the boarded horses that hadn't yet been removed from the farm while Amy had walked around in a daze. But… discussing her love life as if they were jawing over the price of feed corn was embarrassing.

"Yes, I love him," she admitted.

"I expect everythin'll work out."

Swallowing the ache in her throat, she whispered, "Thanks for caring, Jake."

The girls came out of the house, Moose loping after them. Amy lowered the tailgate and the dog vaulted into the truck bed. They drove off, Rose and Lily waving goodbye and Moose's slobbery jowls flapping in the wind.

Twenty minutes later Amy pulled into the ranch yard and her heart screeched to a stop. Matt's truck and horse trailer were missing. Maybe he'd taken the stallion to the equine hospital in Benton. He'd never been clear about why he'd called Nathan last week.

First things first. She'd get the girls settled, then

she'd ring Matt's cell phone and ask what was going on. Inside the house Amy shooed the girls up to their room to play. Moose followed—the dog was no dummy. He'd found the stash of Milk-Bones Rose had hid under her bed. Amy had discovered the dog treats a few days ago when she'd vacuumed the rug in the room.

Once her daughters were occupied, Amy went straight to the phone. As she walked past the kitchen table she spotted the white envelope propped against the fruit bowl and froze. Her name was scrawled in Matt's handwriting across the front.

Dread formed a knot in her stomach. With shaking hands she read the note.

Amy—I know you say you don't want my money, but it's obvious you need help. Before I leave town today, I'm stopping by the bank and paying the mortgage on the farm through September. That should give you enough time to get your finances in order. I've taken SOS with me. Thought I'd save you the trouble of finding a buyer. I'm depositing fifty-thousand into your bank account for the stud. I'll mail you the deposit receipt on my way out of town.

Fifty-thousand dollars?

Use the money to pay off your debts. Keep the rest to buy supplies so you can board horses again.

Tell the girls goodbye for me. Moose, too. I'm going to miss them.

What about her? Wouldn't he miss her?

Obviously not. He'd written nothing else. Tears stained her cheeks and she angrily swiped at them. How dare he believe the worst of her?

Why shouldn't he? You asked him to loan you another mortgage payment, didn't you?

Oh, Lord. Was that the reason Matt had withdrawn after they'd made love in the kitchen? The idea that he truly believed she was using him broke her heart. Amy had been so sure she'd shown Matt her feelings for him were sincere. *But you never told him that you loved him, did you? You never said the words.*

A knock on the door surprised her and for a moment she believed Matt had had a change of heart.

Instead she found Nathan standing on the porch wearing a concerned frown. "Bad news?" he asked.

Ignoring the question, she waved him inside. "What's up?"

"I forgot to tell Matt when I stopped by earlier that there's another test we can run on SOS that might give us a better reading on—"

"You've been running tests on the stallion?"

After a lengthy pause, Nathan asked, "Matt didn't tell you?"

"Tell me what?"

"SOS has testicular degeneration."

"What does that mean?"

"He's sterile."

Her lungs deflated until barely any oxygen squeezed through.

"I'm sorry, Amy. SOS must have suffered an injury to his testicles before Ben purchased him."

Oh, Ben had been so foolish. And Matt, God bless him, had bought SOS because he knew Amy would never be able to sell the stud.

Nathan edged toward the door. "It's a long shot, but we can check SOS's viable sperm and if there's enough we…" The sight of Amy's tears threw the vet. "Have Matt call me." Nathan left, the screen door slamming behind him.

Amy would do better than phone Matt—she'd deliver Nathan's message in person.

She had a few things of her own to say to the stubborn cowboy.

Chapter Fourteen

"Dad sent you out here, didn't he?" Matt glared at his sister, Samantha.

"He's worried about you. So am I." Sam patted his shoulder, then slid a boot across the lower rung of the corral and observed the prancing mares.

When Matt had arrived back in Oklahoma three weeks ago, he'd kept the details of his Idaho trip to himself. He'd been shocked his father hadn't demanded an explanation for the fifty thousand dollars Matt needed to take SOS off Amy's hands. Thank God, because he'd been too embarrassed to explain about the poker game and his dishonest intentions toward another man.

"Have you decided what to do with the stud?" Sam asked. Matt had told his father and his sister SOS was sterile.

"Cole Sanders came over and checked out the horse. Told him I'd sell SOS dirt cheap. The stud will make an excellent ranch horse if someone works with him." Matt was prepared to hand over the animal for free. SOS was a painful reminder of Amy and the girls and he wanted the stud gone yesterday.

Sam arched a black eyebrow. "Does Daddy know a Sanders trespassed on his property?"

"Nope." Neither the Cartwright siblings nor the Sanders siblings knew what had begun the feud between their parents years ago, but Dominick made no apologies for keeping his distance from the neighboring cattle ranch.

"Did Daddy ask you to work for him?"

"Yep." Two separate conversations, neither lasting more than five minutes. Matt refused to become a corporate cowboy. He liked his callused hands and outdoor tan just fine. "Told him no thanks, like I always do."

"None of us kids loves oil the way he does." Sam added, "Maybe we inherited our love for cattle and horses from our mother."

"Maybe." He studied his sister's profile. She was a striking woman with a soft heart. He'd quit setting her up with his rodeo buddies years ago—the dates had triggered panic attacks, which had made her memory lapses more glaring. One day Matt hoped a man would come along determined enough to break through the stone wall Sam had erected around her.

"What about your dream to breed cutting horses?"

"Those plans are on hold." Matt was ashamed that his selfish greed had caused him to act so recklessly. He should have investigated SOS's history before hauling the mares all the way to Idaho and Amy's ranch. He was as much an idiot as Ben Olson in that department.

If you had, you'd never have met Amy.

"I'm heading out on the circuit in a few days." He'd rope calves for however long it took to pay his father back.

"This past Christmas you talked about retiring from rodeo."

That was before he'd screwed up everything. "Plans change."

"Do your new plans have anything to do with a woman?"

Sam's whispered question stung like a slap across the cheek. He hadn't told a soul about Amy—not even his father. "What gives you the idea I'm involved with a woman?"

"I've never seen you mope before."

After Matt had broken up with Kayla, he'd stayed on the road for nearly six months—until he'd had his emotions under control and felt sane enough to join his family at the ranch. Raw from leaving Amy and the girls, Matt must not have hid his feelings very well.

"Her name's Amy." He'd held everything inside him since leaving the Broken Wheel. The need to talk won out. He and Sam had a special bond—one forged when their mother had abandoned them. They knew things about each other that their father wasn't even aware of—for instance, Sam's horrible nightmares that occurred once a month like clockwork.

"Amy's husband owned SOS." The talking part was more difficult than Matt anticipated.

"And…"

"And it's a big mess. Of my own doing." Matt removed his cowboy hat and wiped a shirtsleeve across his sweaty brow. The beginning of July had ushered in ninety-degree temperatures and plenty of humidity. "I appreciate the shoulder, Sam, but…" His voice trailed off at the hurt that flashed through his sister's eyes. Since Sam's accident years ago he and the rest of the family had made a habit of sparing unpleasant news from her—for her own protection. She often forgot or confused facts, which upset her.

"Will you keep this between you and me?" At her solemn nod he continued. "Amy's husband was a bronc rider on the circuit." In case Sam had forgotten the story he'd told the family at Christmas, he refreshed her memory. "Ben and I got into a card game in Pocatello this past December and he lost to me. Big-time. He didn't have the funds to pay up, so I accepted stud fees in lieu of cash."

"Go on," Sam urged when Matt became lost in the memory of that night at the arena.

"Ben never showed up with the stud, so—"

"You took the mares to Idaho," Sam concluded.

"When I got to the horse farm I learned Ben had died."

Sam gasped. "What happened?"

Did he dare tell his sister the truth? "SOS kicked him in the chest and the blow killed him."

His sister's face paled and Matt grabbed her arm, fearing she'd faint. "Damn it, I should have kept my mouth shut." The last thing he wished for Sam was for her to relive her own nightmare of being kicked by a horse.

"I'm okay." She smiled bravely, then glanced toward the barn. "Why did you bring the stud here if he's vicious?"

"He's not a killer. He's terrified of rats. The best I

can figure is that a rat got into the stall when Ben was in with the stud and the horse went berserk."

"That's so sad."

"When I arrived at the Broken Wheel I discovered that Ben had been married and had two daughters."

Sam's eyes narrowed. "Matt Cartwright, I hope you didn't take advantage of a newly widowed woman."

"It wasn't like that at all. Amy and Ben's marriage hadn't been the best. She was through mourning her husband when I arrived."

"Then you love her?" Sam's question came out of the blue.

"Amy isn't anything like the women I normally date."

"I should say not. She has children."

"Amy's husband left her with a ton of debt and a sterile stud."

"Oh, Matt," Sam whispered. "You bought SOS to help her out, didn't you?"

Did all women have this uncanny ability to read a man's mind? "Amy doesn't know about the stallion's sterility. If she did, she wouldn't have accepted my money."

"I don't understand. If you love her, why aren't you together? Is it because you don't want kids?"

"Not at all. Rose and Lily are cute as can be."

Sam's eyes darkened. "She doesn't love you, does she?"

He swallowed hard. "I'm pretty sure she loves me." But she shouldn't. He wasn't worthy of her love.

"Then what's the problem?" Sam smacked her hand against his back. "Be together and be happy."

If it were that simple…

"Mind if I join you two?" Dominick Cartwright approached the corral and Matt wondered how much of the conversation his father had overheard.

"I'm heading inside to help Juanita bake cookies." Sam leaned in and kissed Matt's cheek, then walked off.

Silence settled between the two men and finally Matt caved first. "If you've got something to say, go ahead."

"Pride can change a man's life forever."

The comment confirmed that his father had heard Matt mention Amy. "What's your point, Dad?"

"I should have gone after Charlotte as soon as she left me. I'm afraid I set a bad example."

His father rarely spoke about his first wife. Matt didn't remember his mother at all. He had fonder memories of his father's second wife and the various housekeepers and ranch hands over the years.

"I loved her and I should have searched for her. But I was hurt by her affair."

Affair? Infidelity had destroyed his parents' marriage.

"I was cocky and full of myself and believed your mother would come crawling home—if not for me, then for my money. Weeks turned into years and no word from Charlotte. Then one day I woke up and realized your mother was never coming home." His father cleared his throat. "Charlotte and I might have worked things out if I'd swallowed my pride and tracked her down."

Matt wished it was a simple matter of infidelity between him and Amy. Sometimes he wished Amy had been another Kayla and had had an affair on him. Forgiving her would be a hell of a lot easier than asking for her forgiveness.

"If she doesn't fall for your handsome mug or your buckles, then she ought to fall for our oil wells." His father grinned.

Matt chuckled, but the ache inside him split his chest apart. Amy didn't give a flip about Cartwright Oil. "Thanks for the advice, Dad. I'll sleep on it."

"What do you plan to do with the stud?"

"Sell him. Cole Sanders is interested." His father's mouth tightened and Matt rushed to change the subject. "I'll be heading out on the circuit next week."

"What happened to hanging up the ropes for good?"

"That was before I took out a loan from you."

"Forget about the money, son." His father adjusted the Stetson on his head. "I shouldn't have put conditions on your trust fund. I can't say I'm thrilled that none of my kids want to join me in the oil business, but if raising horses is what you want to do with your life, then let's discuss it."

Matt was humbled by his father's support in light of the fact that the old man had detested horses since the day Sam had nearly been killed by one. "Dad, that's really generous of you, but—"

"We've got company," his father said, watching a plume of dust form in the distance.

A few seconds later Matt recognized the rattletrap and sucked in a quiet breath. *Amy.* His heart pounded first with excitement, then with frustration. The woman was nuts to drive all the way to Tulsa in a truck with no air-conditioning, old tires and a busted radio.

When the vehicle slowed near the corrals, Rose waved her arms out the window. "Mr. Matt! Mr. Matt!" The little girl's greeting was followed by a *woof* from the truck bed. Moose's tail waved like a flyswatter at a watermelon-eating contest.

The porch door squeaked open and Sam joined Matt and their father at the corral. "Wow," she said. "A ready-made family."

Matt ignored his father's raised eyebrow and savored the feeling of hope filling him. Amy got out of the truck and glared across the hood. Her tight-lipped mouth and stiff shoulders barely registered with Matt, but the soft, flyaway curls framing her pretty face held his attention. Even from a distance he remembered the sweet smell of her shampoo and the scent of her skin.

A low whistle escaped Sam's mouth. "She's ticked. What did you do to her, big brother?"

Amy's courage stumbled when the beautiful woman joined Matt and the older man. *Stop that.* It didn't matter anymore what Matt had or had not felt for her. She'd come for one reason and one reason only—to have the final say in their relationship—that is if one called what they'd had these past few weeks a relationship.

She strolled around the hood and opened the passenger-side door. Rose bolted. Lily lifted her arms in the air and as soon as Amy set her on the ground she toddled after her sister, her sippy cup waving in the air, juice flying everywhere. Amy then lowered the tailgate and Moose jumped to the ground. He loped toward Matt, passing by Lily so fast he spun her in a circle.

"Mr. Matt! Mr. Matt!" Rose dove for Matt and he scooped her into his arms. "You didn't say goodbye," she accused, hugging his neck.

Not to be outdone by her sister, Lily called, "Mer Matt! Mer Matt!" Then she grabbed Matt around one leg and smiled shyly up at the dark-haired woman. Moose followed, standing on his hind legs, he pawed Matt's chest and slobbered on his shirt.

"You must be Matt's father, Dominick Cartwright," Amy said, joining the group. A striking man with his head of white hair and dark eyebrows and dark mustache. "Amy Olson, from Pebble Creek, Idaho." She shook hands, surprised when Matt's father held her fingers longer than necessary, studying her face as if trying to read her mind. "These are my girls, Rose and Lily. That monster is Moose." She pointed to the dog.

"I'm Samantha, Matt's sister." The dark-haired beauty smiled at the girls. "Hi, Rose. Hi, Lily."

Amy noticed Samantha had looked at the wrong girl when she'd called them by name, but her daughters didn't care.

Matt's sister must have sensed a storm brewing because she suggested, "How would you girls like to head up to the house and help Juanita in the kitchen? She's baking cookies and I bet she'll let you have one."

"Can we, Mama?" Rose asked.

The girls had missed Matt like crazy the past couple of weeks. Amy's eyes shifted to Matt's hand, which rested protectively against Lily's blond curls and her throat tightened. "Sure." The word came out a whisper. Embarrassed, she cleared her throat and spoke louder. "Mind your manners."

Samantha held their hands as they walked off, Moose trailing behind.

"Welcome to the Lazy River, Mrs. Olson. I hope you and your daughters will be our guests for dinner tonight."

"I'll let you know later. You might rescind the invitation after I speak with your son."

Mr. Cartwright's eyes rounded, then filled with a devilish sparkle. "Fair enough." With a tip of his hat, he sauntered off.

As soon as his father was out of hearing range Matt said, "I'm sorry."

"Don't." Amy held a hand up, then cursed the burning sensation in her eyes. The sound of his voice was enough to remind her to keep her guard up and not allow the cowboy to sneak under her radar.

"I'm not here to beg you to come back to me and the girls." She paused in the middle of drawing a breath when Matt's tan face turned pasty. *Had he thought… What was he…* "And I am most certainly not here to beg you to love me." The sadness in his blue eyes took the steam out of her mad and confused her. "I came here to tell you that I'm not after your money."

She removed a folded check from her jean pocket and slapped it against his chest, leaving him no choice but to accept it or let it fall to the ground. "That covers what you paid me for SOS and five months' worth of mortgage payments."

After reading the amount on the bank draft, he frowned.

"I'm not Kayla."

Matt stiffened. "Who told you about Kayla?"

"You did." Face heating with embarrassment, she admitted, "The day you got kicked by SOS, I overheard you talking to Lily when you were soaking in the tub."

"You misunderstood."

"I don't believe so. And I came here to set the record straight. When Jake disclosed the information about your father's wealth, never once did I think about cozying up to you in hopes of getting my hands on the Cartwright fortune." Her throat went dry. "All I want is to keep my home and care for my daughters. I've never been afraid of hard work or little dirt beneath my fingernails. And taking that darn data-entry job should have proved how far I'm willing to go to secure my girls' futures."

"Amy, I never—"

"Let me finish." If she didn't get it all out now she never would. "I was going to tell you this the night in the kitchen after we—" she held his gaze "—had sex." He winced and Amy experienced a momentary prick of satisfaction. She'd believed they'd been making love, but figured Matt had considered it nothing more than the down-'n'-dirty. "It took time to check into the claim's legitimacy."

"What claim?" he asked.

"My father kept a notebook of get-rich-quick schemes. He suspected the farm's soil contained the mineral phosphate." Matt didn't interrupt, so she continued. "My father died before any surveys had been conducted."

"I suppose that prick of a bank manager knew about the phosphate," Matt said.

"That's why Payton wanted me to sell." She cleared her throat. "I had a geological survey done shortly after you left. The results came in a couple of days ago."

"And…?"

"There's phosphate in the ground. Plenty of it." She offered a small smile. "The check won't bounce."

Matt's eyes glazed over as he stared into space. Amy shivered despite the warm wind. "Oh, God," she whispered, pressing her fingers against her mouth. "You didn't leave because of the money, did you?"

Bleak blue eyes settled on her face. "No."

Pain sliced through her chest, piercing her heart. Had she misread his actions? "You really don't love me." Tears blinded her. The girls... She had to get the girls and Moose and leave before she fell at Matt's feet and begged him to... *Love me.*

"You're wrong, Amy." Hoarse emotion coated each word when he spoke and she didn't have the strength to look away from his handsome face. "I left *because* I love you," he insisted.

"I don't understand."

Shoving a hand through his hair, he shuffled sideways, putting more distance between them. Amy struggled not to lose hope.

"I wanted you to believe I left because I thought you were after my money."

"Why?"

"Because if I told you the truth about the poker game in Pocatello *you'd* stop loving *me.*"

"I never said I loved you, Matt," she pointed out.

"Maybe not with words. But you said it when you touched me. When you whispered in my ear and breathed against my neck. When you took me inside you."

Heart melting, she whispered, "I'm listening."

Damn it, telling the truth shouldn't be this difficult...this painful. Matt would rather suffer the effects of a mean-faced rodeo bull whipping him around like a rag doll than confess his sin to the woman he loved.

The woman he'd given his heart to.

The woman he wanted to spend the rest of his life with.

"Every cowboy on the circuit was aware of Ben's gambling addiction, including me." Matt swallowed hard. "I'm not going to pretty it up, Amy. I suckered Ben into a card game because I knew I'd win and he wouldn't be able to pay up."

"Why would you do that?"

"I'd heard that he owned Son of Sunshine. I knew about the stud and decided he'd be perfect for my mares. So I made sure Ben lost a lot of money and then I offered to cancel his debt to me in exchange for SOS's stud services."

Matt examined the ground for a long time—until the blurring dust settled. Then he stared Amy square in the eye. "I keep telling myself that if I had known he was married and had kids I would never have put him in that position. But I can't say for sure it would have made a difference. I was determined to retire from rodeo and go into the horse-breeding business and I doubt anything would have stopped me that night."

He forced himself to stay put when he'd rather walk off.

"All those nice things you did…babysitting the girls…the money you loaned me…Moose…was out of guilt?"

"Don't you get it, Amy? If I hadn't coaxed Ben into that card game—"

"Some other cowboy would have, Matt," Amy argued.

"That doesn't excuse my behavior, and then to top it off, I had the audacity to fall in love with the widow of the man I wronged."

"If I wasn't already a widow when you'd arrived at the farm, Matt, I was on my way to becoming a divorcée." After a dramatic sigh, she said, "I'm probably going to say this all wrong, but first let me assure you that I truly grieved over Ben's death. Not as a woman who'd lost her soul mate or her beloved husband. I grieved over Ben losing his life in such a senseless way."

"I don't understand."

"Ben was the father of my children, but there was no abiding love between us. We never had a strong marriage and he died before I got up the nerve to tell him I'd contacted a lawyer to file for a divorce."

Amy was mistaken if she believed her planning to divorce Ben would ease his guilt.

"Matt, whether you and I work out or not, you must accept the fact that Ben had a gambling addiction. That was his problem. His responsibility—not yours."

"But I'm a better man than I showed myself to be that night in Pocatello. I'm not proud of my actions. I wasn't raised to take advantage of other people."

"No one's perfect, Matt. If I would have allowed Rose to get a dog a while back then maybe Ben wouldn't have—"

"The rat would have remained in the barn whether Rose had a dog or not."

After a stretch of silence, Amy said, "It's time we both forgive ourselves and move on. I don't profess to have all the answers to life's questions, but maybe the reason for Ben's death is as simple as…it was his time to go."

"Maybe," Matt admitted. "But that doesn't entitle me to what belonged to him."

"Ben never wanted me or the girls, or else he'd have treated us better."

Matt struggled to absorb the words and make sense of them. Maybe Ben hadn't loved Amy the way he should have, but Matt was sure the man had appreciated his daughters. He glanced toward the house where Rose and Lily had gone. He loved the two little girls as if they'd been born his. Wouldn't Ben want his daughters to have a father who loved them?

Would loving Amy and the girls be enough to make amends for his sins? God, he hoped so because he didn't have the strength to walk away from them. "I love you, Amy. I love Rose and Lily, too. If you can forgive me for what I did to Ben, then I want us to be a family."

He waited for Amy to throw herself into his arms, but she didn't. His heart stopped beating. Was it too late? Had he screwed things up so badly that she refused to give him a second chance?

"If you're proposing because you feel guilty, I won't marry you." She propped her fists on her hips. For all her bravado, Amy failed to hide the love for him in her eyes.

He'd be a fool to walk away from a future with this woman and her daughters. As if gentling a skittish filly, Matt caressed Amy's cheek, rubbing his thumb back and forth. "I'm proposing because I love you and I don't want to live without you and the girls." He leaned his forehead against hers and breathed in her subtle scent.

"We're not very good at saying the words, are we?" she whispered, nuzzling her nose along his cheek.

"We'll get better."

"I'm sorry that woman hurt you so badly, Matt."

"I'm not." He brushed a fleeting kiss across his lips. "If I hadn't been wronged, I'd have never discovered real love." Another kiss. "The real love that's standing right here in front of me."

Amy cuddled against Matt, wrapping her arms around his waist. "I love you, Matt. And it's not because you're—" she smiled "—a *hottie,* as Rose's bus driver claims."

Hottie? Good God, he hoped his siblings didn't get wind of that nickname. He'd never live it down.

"I fell in love with you," she continued, her quiet words a balm to his battered soul, "because you bought Silly Nillys at the grocery store for the girls. Because you picked up Lily's marbles off the bathroom floor. Because you cared enough about Rose's secret pet to try and trap Sophia instead of using poison to get rid of her. Because you bought Moose to heal Rose's broken heart. Because you paid for a sterile stud so I'd have a fighting chance to keep my farm." She paused to take a deep breath. "But you know why I love you most of all?"

He shook his head.

"Because you make my heart sing. The grass looks greener. The sun burns hotter. My flowers bloom longer. You make my world so much brighter and richer."

"If you give me the chance, Amy, I promise I'll show you every day, every hour, every minute how much I love you and the girls."

"I'll give you more than a chance, Matt. I'll give you forever."

"MAMA'S KISSING MR. MATT," Rose announced from her post at the door.

"Mer Matt. Mer Matt." Lily clanged her sippy cup against the screen.

Dominick joined the girls, lifting Lily up and propping her on his hip. "Now you can see better." He and the girls watched the couple's embrace.

Guess my son has found himself a new family. Dominick was both sad and happy. One by one his children were leaving the nest.

"Another wedding is on the horizon," Samantha murmured, peering around her father's shoulder. She stroked Lily's blond curls. "You're such a cutie."

Lily grinned around the mouthpiece of her sippy cup.

"My sister poops in her pants. That's not very cute," Rose said.

Dominick chuckled. "Rose, you and I are going to get along fine."

"Okay. If you say so." She opened the door and stepped onto the porch. "I'm going see if Mama's gonna marry Mr. Matt."

"Would you like Mr. Matt to be your father?" Dominick asked.

The little girl's hazel eyes sparkled. "Oh, yeah. He's the best. He never told Mama about Sophia."

"Who's Sophia?" Samantha spoke.

"She was my pet rat. But SOS squashed her. That's why Mr. Matt got us Moose."

Lily squirmed in Dominick's arms and he set her on her feet. She followed her sister outside.

"Idaho's a long ways away," Dominick murmured.

"So is Detroit, Daddy, and you've gone to visit Duke and Renée twice since they married."

Dominick wrapped an arm around his daughter. One day soon he hoped Samantha would find her own happy ever after. He smiled as his soon-to-be granddaughters and their sidekick, Moose, raced toward the corral. The group hugged, their laughter and the dog's barking stirring up more dust than an Oklahoma twister.

* * * * *

Be sure to look for Marin Thomas's next book,
SAMANTHA'S COWBOY.
Available in August 2009
wherever Harlequin books are sold.

*Celebrate 60 years of pure
reading pleasure with Harlequin®!*

*Step back in time and enjoy
a sneak preview of an exciting anthology
from Harlequin® Historical with*
THE DIAMONDS OF WELBOURNE MANOR

This compelling anthology features three stories
about the outrageous Fitzmanning sisters. Meet
Annalise, who is never at a loss for words… But
that can change with an unexpected encounter in
the forest.

*Available May 2009
from Harlequin® Historical.*

"I'm the illegitimate daughter of notoriously scandalous parents, Mr. Milford. Candidates for my hand are unlikely to be lining up at the gates."

"Don't be so quick to discount your charms, my dear. Or the charm of your substantial dowry. Or even your brothers' influence. There are as many reasons to marry as there are marriages."

Annalise snorted. "Oh, yes. Perhaps I shall marry for dynastic reasons, or perhaps for property or influence. After all, a loveless, practical marriage worked out so well for my mother."

"Well, you've routed me on that one. I can think of no suitable rejoinder." Ned rose to his feet and extended his hand. "And since that is the case, let me be the first to wish you a long and happy spinsterhood."

Her mouth gaped open. And then she laughed.

And he froze.

This was the first time, Ned realized. The first time he'd seen her eyes light up and her mouth curl. The first time he'd witnessed her features melded together in glorious accord to produce exquisite beauty.

Unbelievable what a change came over her face. Unheard of what effect her throaty, rasping laughter had on his body. It pounded a beat upon his ear, quickly taken up by his pulse. It echoed through him, finally residing in his stirring nether regions.

So easily she did it, awakened these sensations within him—without any apparent effort at all. And she had called him potentially dangerous? Clearly the intelligent thing for him to do would be to steer clear, to leave her to the tender ministrations of Lord Peter Blackthorne.

"You were right." She smiled up at him as she took his hand and climbed to her feet. "I do feel better."

Ah, well. When had he ever chosen the intelligent path?

He did not relinquish her hand. He used it to pull her in, close enough that he could feel the warmth of her. "At the risk of repeating Lord Peter's mistake and anticipating too much—may I ask if you'll be my partner in battledore tomorrow?"

Her smiled dimmed. Her breath came a little faster. His own had gone shallow, as if he'd just run a race— and lost. He ran his gaze over the appealing lift of her brow and the curious angle of her chin. His index finger twitched.

"I should like that," she said.

His finger trembled again and he lifted it, traced the pink and tender shell of her ear, the unique sweep of her jaw. Her pulse leaped beneath her skin, triggering his own. Slowly he tilted her chin up, waiting for her to object, to step back, to slap his hand away.

She did none of those eminently sensible things. Which left him free to do the entirely impractical thing.

Baby soft, the skin of her lips. Her whole body trembled when he touched her there.

He leaned in. Her eyes closed, even as she stood straight against him, strung as tight as a bow. He pressed his mouth to hers. It was a soft kiss, sweet and chaste. And yet he was hot and hard and as ready as he'd ever been in his life.

She drew back a little. Sighed. Their breath mingled a moment before she slowly backed away.

"Oh," she breathed. Her dark eyes were full of wonder and something that looked like fear. He took a step toward her, but she only shook her head. His outstretched hand fell to his side as she turned to disappear into the wood. This was the first time, Ned realized. The first time, since he'd come to the house party at Welbourne Manor, that he'd seen her eyes light up.

* * * * *

Follow Ned and Annalise's story in May 2009 in
THE DIAMONDS OF WELBOURNE MANOR
Available May 2009
from Harlequin® Historical

Available in the series romance section,
or in the historical romance section,
wherever books are sold.